The Malthusian Correction

JG Faherty

Lycan Valley Press Publications
1002 N Meridian STE 100-153
Puyallup, Washington 98371
United States of America

First Edition

ISBN-13: 978-1-64562-039-6

The Malthusian Correction is a book that owes a debt of gratitude to many people.

My wife, Andrea, for always supporting everything I do. My mom, Teresa, for avidly reading everything I write—again and again! The team at Lycan Valley Press Publications, including MJae Sydney and her staff, for doing such a great job with my books.

My friends in NY, who I miss, and my friends in NC, who I am glad to have found. The Malthusian Correction was the last book I ever wrote in my old office in NY, and in a way it mirrors my move south and my major life transformation (although, as far as I know, I have not died or caused a religious upheaval!).

Finally, I want to say thank you to all the writers and editors who have helped get me to this place—especially my beta readers!—your aid has been invaluable..

The
Malthusian
Correction

T HE URGE HIT Roger Brenner in the middle of the football game.

I should go for a walk.

Roger stood up, his old recliner complaining more than his forty-five-year-old bones. Potato chip crumbs tumbled from his lap, but he paid no attention. On the big flat screen TV he'd brought home last Christmas, the Dolphins had just scored another touchdown over the Giants, but the game no longer held any importance.

"Get me a soda, will you?" Marcie flicked her eyes in his direction for a moment before turning back to the TV. She had the newspaper propped against her knees. A chronic multitasker, she usually worked on a crossword or Sudoku during the commercials. Ben and Patty sat on the other couch, so immersed in the videos streaming on their tablets they didn't even look up.

"I'm not going upstairs," Roger said. "I'm going

for a walk."

"A walk? It's not even halftime."

"That's okay. I must've sat around too much today. I gotta stretch the old legs." In fact, he didn't feel that way at all. But he also couldn't find the right words to describe his sudden need to move, to leave one place and go to another.

To *walk*.

"Where are you going?"

"I don't know. Around the block, maybe. Down to the store. Somewhere. Do me good to get some exercise."

"Well, have a good time."

"Okay, hon. See you later."

On his way out the back door, Roger grabbed his blue New York Giants zip-up sweatshirt, the one with the fleece lining, from the coat rack. Bright September sunshine greeted him as he stepped outside, the light just taking on the deeper yellow of late afternoon. The smell of early fall, so different from even late summer, lingered in the warm air and Roger took an appreciative breath as he headed down the driveway. With his sweatshirt over one shoulder and his other hand in his pocket, he turned left onto Mulberry Lane, which went through several cookie-cutter neighborhoods until it stopped at Central Avenue after a mile.

"Hey, Rog!"

Roger nodded and smiled at Eddie Backman, who had one hand lifted in greeting as he wheeled a fertilizer spreader across his front yard.

"Rog, you wanna come over and have a—"

The rest of Eddie's words disappeared.

No time to stop in for a beer. Sorry. Taking a walk. Walking. Walking.

Half a block later, he didn't remember leaving the house or seeing his neighbor.

All that mattered was walking.

At the end of Central Avenue, Roger turned left, heading east on Route 210. The sun sat just above the horizon, a fiery globe painting the clouds in reds and oranges and warming the back of his neck. Roger kept to the shoulder, gravel crunching underfoot while cars whizzed by on the four-lane road, stirring up dust in their passing. Sweat and grime coated his face, but he didn't bother to wipe it away, even when it dripped into his eyes. Although he'd walked four miles since leaving his house, his feet didn't ache and his legs felt as fresh as when he'd started.

Might as well keep going. I never realized walking was so easy. I should do this more often. Walk. Walking. Walking.

"Go tell your father dinner's ready." Marcie Brenner took a quick taste of the chili and smacked her lips. Just the right hint of fiery spice, but not so much that it overwhelmed the flavors of meat and tomato.

"Dad! Dinner's ready!"

"I said go tell him, not announce it to the whole

neighborhood."

"Okay." Ben sat down at the table, already lost again in whatever game he had going on his phone. Marcie considered scolding him, then decided against it. You had to pick your battles with teenagers, and this ranked pretty low on the list of importance. She set a steaming bowl of chili in front of him and placed a bag of corn tortilla chips and a jar of salsa on the table. While she ladled more chili in to bowls, Patty came in and sat down.

"Where's Dad?"

Route 210 cut a straight line through Rocky Point from the Palisades Parkway entrance at the west end of town to Route 9W at the east end, which Roger reached a little before seven p.m., three hours after leaving his house. At the intersection, he turned right, following 9W southeast. Despite it being a Sunday, traffic flowed at a steady pace, a combination of locals heading to or from bars and restaurants and out of towners on their way back to New York or Westchester or New Jersey after a day upstate picking apples or visiting wineries. A couple of drivers recognized Roger and honked their horns. Each time, Roger lifted his hand and gave a little wave.

And then promptly forgot about them.

Two more miles brought him to Halloran's Ice Cream, where a few families and couples stood in line waiting for cones or sundaes despite the growing chill in the air. The neon sign burned bright pink against the night sky, and the giant plastic cone on the roof, as much a Rocky Point landmark as any of the historic buildings in town, rotated slowly around, the same way it had done every day from May 1st to September 31st-for the past fifty years.

Although he hadn't eaten in close to six hours, Roger's stomach didn't growl as he passed the shop and crossed over into the town of Haverstraw. A pleasant humming filled his head, a mental white noise that both calmed and energized him. He passed several streets, stopping only when he had to wait for traffic lights to change from red to green. Whenever this happened, he walked in place, legs moving up and down in exactly the same rhythm as when he was actually striding forward.

At one corner, he slipped on his sweatshirt, zipping it just enough to keep it from flapping open. Hands tucked in his pockets, he started up the long, gradual slope to where 9W exited the center of town and continued on east. Headlights flashed by and the occasional passing truck blew his hair around and peppered him with grit.

He didn't notice. The white noise shielded him from outside distractions. His body operated on autopilot, leaving his brain to focus on the one thing that remained important.

Walking. Walking. Waaalkkkkinggggggggg…

"9-1-1. What is your emergency?"

Marcie Brenner bit her lip and swallowed back a sob before she could reply. *Emergency? My fucking husband's disappeared, you bitch!* she wanted to shout, but she managed to control her emotions enough to speak.

"I… I want to report a missing person. My husband."

"What is your name and address, ma'am?"

Marcie provided it, and then Roger's name as well when the operator asked. Then she stamped her foot in frustration when the emotionless voice told her to wait and she'd be connected to her local police barrack.

I could've just called there myself!

Four hours. Maybe longer. She hadn't been paying attention to the clock when Roger said he was stepping out for a stroll. Almost halftime in the game, she remembered that much.

Roger, where the hell are you?

The last hour was a jumble of images. Searching the house, thinking he'd come back and was taking a nap or puttering around in the garage, or maybe outside chatting with one of the neighbors. Sharing a beer and stupidly unaware of the commotion he was causing. Then irritation morphing into the first seedlings of fear. Had he fallen somewhere? Been hit by a car? Had a heart attack?

She'd driven around the neighborhood and then expanded her search to several streets in both directions. There'd been no sign of him. By the time she'd returned home, fear had a solid grip on her stomach and she'd dialed 9-1-1 while Ben and Patty sat on the couch, their faces mirroring the dread growing inside her. She wanted to comfort them, tell them everything would be okay.

More than that, she wanted someone to do the same thing for her.

Because that nagging voice in her head was whispering to her that everything wasn't okay, something terrible had happened, their lives were about to change for the worse.

Goddamn you, Roger. When I find you, you're gonna wish you were—

"Rocky Point Police, Officer Larson speaking."

"Oh!" Lost in her musings, she'd almost forgotten she was on hold. "Hello. This is Marcie Brenner. My husband is missing."

"Alright, Mrs. Brenner. What makes you think he's missing?" The officer's voice was soft and pleasant, which had the opposite effect he probably intended. Rather than calming her, it grated on her nerves, adding frustration to the mix of emotions already boiling within her.

She told him everything that had happened.

"Okay. Are you sure he's not at a neighbor's house? Did you try calling him?"

"Of course I did! I'm not an idiot. He didn't take

his phone with him, it's right by his chair where he left it."

"All right, calm down, Mrs. Brenner. I'll send an officer over. Someone should be there in a few minutes."

"Thank you."

Then it was just a matter of waiting. The three of them sitting and staring at each other, at the walls, at nothing. The living room no longer felt like home. Normally full of noise—the TV, voices, music from phones or pads—now a heavy silence reigned, so total she could hear her own pulse in her ears and the whisper of Ben breathing next to her. Even the children were acting different. Neither of them had their phones out.

If teenagers are worried, it has to be serious.

Thinking that certainly didn't help her—

Ding-DING-Ding!

Marcie gasped and jumped at the doorbell's chime. Patty let out a startled "Oh!" and Benny ran to the window.

"It's the police!"

Her heart pounding, Marcie hurried to the door. Two officers with serious faces waited on the porch. Both were in their thirties and about six feet tall, with athletic builds. One had a mustache, the short, thick, Freddie Mercury kind she and Roger had always laughingly called the "cop 'stache."

Tonight she wasn't laughing.

"Mrs. Brenner? I'm Officer Gregg," said the

mustached man. "And this is Officer Torrey. You reported your husband missing?"

"Yes, please come in."

It took ten minutes for her to tell the story a third time, and then another fifteen to answer the officers' questions. These were more detailed than what the officer on the phone had asked. She had to give the names of their neighbors and friends, details about Roger's job and his after-work habits. Toward the end, Torrey cleared his throat and rather sheepishly asked if there were any problems in the home.

"Of course not! We weren't fighting, we were watching football. He said he wanted to stretch his legs, that was all."

"Sorry, ma'am, but we have to ask. What about money troubles? Any issues at work?"

"My dad is an accountant," Patty said. "He's been at the same company since before I was born."

"Hush." Marcie motioned for Patty to sit back down and then turned her eyes back to the officers. "My daughter's right, though. Roger's got a good job at Wallace and Fender. He's well-respected there and he loves his work. We're not in any kind of financial trouble. Instead of asking me these questions, shouldn't you be out looking for him? Or checking the hospitals? He could be—"

She caught herself before her next words "dying someplace" came out, remembering Ben and Patty at the last moment. Instead, she finished with "—hurt, with no way to get in touch with us."

"We'll do all of that, ma'am, and more. But we need as much information as we can get in order to know how to best start our investigation. Now, do you have a picture handy?"

"Of course." She pulled one up on her phone. She'd taken it just a few days earlier, Roger standing by the grill out back as he cooked dinner. The officer asked her to text it to him, and then said they would begin checking all the standard places.

"Hospitals, bus stations, train stations. Even airports. We'll also call or visit everyone on the list you gave us."

"And what are we supposed to do?" Marcie asked, as the officers headed for the door.

"Sit tight. He might call. We'll definitely keep you updated. And you make sure to do the same. If you hear anything from him, from relatives, from friends, let us know right away."

Then they were gone.

Marcie looked at her children. They stared back and then both of them burst into tears.

A second later, Marcie joined them.

The sky was black and clouds hid the stars as Roger found himself walking up the long, steep incline that marked the beginning of a sort of no-man's land between Haverstraw and the next town over, Congers. For the next mile there was only the road, a strip of county parkland that sat between the

Hudson River and 9W on his left, and the jagged, rocky face of High Tor Mountain.

No sidewalk existed here, and the shoulder on either side was barely four feet wide. Cars and trucks sped by at better than fifty-five miles per hour, creating a deadly environment for anyone foolish enough to walk the road, especially at night.

Roger never flinched, not even when a semi loaded with gravel from the nearby quarry practically blew him off his feet as it passed.

By then he'd walked over eight miles. Sweat coated his body, turning to thin mud where it mixed with road dust and grit. His legs and hips moved in a steady rhythm, one foot and then the other, automatically compensating his balance as he went up or down hills.

Random thoughts flittered through his head, appearing and disappearing, like leaves skittering across the road in a breeze.

This feels right.

Walking. Walking.

Must get to the place.

Walking.

Images of Marcie, Ben, and Patty popped up and then vanished. Always smiling. Each time, a feeling of warmth and comfort filled him. He loved his family, they loved him. What could be better?

Not once did he wonder what they were doing, if they were worried.

He was walking. He had a destination to reach,

although he didn't know yet where it was. He would know it when he needed to. That was all that mattered.

Up the hill, down the long, gentle slope on the other side. In another mile, he came to a fork in the road. 9W veered to the left and Route 304 went straight.

Roger took the turn without pausing, staying on 9W. A few hundred yards brought him into Congers proper. Some garages and shops on his right, a small condo complex to the left. The shoulder was wider here and he unconsciously moved as far from the road as it allowed.

As he rounded another curve, the breeze picked up and he zipped his sweatshirt all the way.

Walking. Walking.

Forward.

I have a purpose.

Walking.

"No word from any of the hospitals or emergency health centers. That's good news. We've still got the alerts out for him, and every cop from here to Jersey is on the lookout. We'll find him, don't worry."

"Thank you." Marcie Brenner hung up the phone and squeezed her eyes shut to stave off another round of tears.

Good news? Maybe Officer Torrey thought so, but it didn't do much to make her feel better. Roger could still be dead or dying in a ditch somewhere and they just hadn't found him yet.

"We'll find him, don't worry." Ha. How was she supposed to not worry? He'd been gone almost six hours. Six hours! Did the cops really believe they'd locate him in the dark? They didn't even know which direction he'd gone when he left.

She glanced into the living room. Ben and Patty were on the couch, staring at the TV. Even from a room away she could see the toll their father's disappearance had already taken. Their eyes were red from crying, their lips were pressed tight. The blue-white glow of the TV washed the color from their faces, making the shadows already forming under their eyes even more noticeable. Patty kept looking at her phone. She'd sent private messages to all her friends, hoping social media could do what the police couldn't: deliver news of her father's whereabouts.

Marcie sipped her fourth coffee of the night, grimacing as the bitter liquid mixed with the acid churning in her stomach. What she really wanted was a glass of wine. Or an edible. But she had to stay awake. There'd be no sleeping until her husband was found.

Goddamn you, Roger. Why? Why did you do this?

Just like every time she'd asked the question tonight, no answer appeared.

Welcome to Nyack

Roger passed the sign without it registering in his conscious mind. He was

Walking. Walking.

focused on the road in front of him, his heart beating in perfect synchronization with his footsteps.

Thump-thump-thump-thump.

Walk-ing. Walk-ing.

When he came to a sidewalk, the first one since he'd left Rocky Point more than eleven miles ago, he stepped onto it, unconsciously adjusting his steps to avoid cracks and to not trip when the cement dipped or he reached a curb.

Walking. Walking.

Although the temperature had dropped into the fifties, he no longer felt the cold. He'd also stopped sweating. A half-hour earlier he'd pissed a little into his pants but it had mostly dried now.

He passed rows of grand houses, mansions from another time. Then he came to a newer section of town, where the homes were more modest ranches and colonials. Many were already dark, the families in bed because tomorrow was Monday, there was work and school.

He passed a strip mall and a hospital. *Walking. Walking.* An intersection with a red light, where he stopped, his legs still moving up and down, waiting for the signal to change. The moment it turned green, he crossed the street. Up a short hill and down, two blocks, and then he reached another light, this time marking the point where 9W met another major road, Route 59.

Had Roger been aware of anything, he'd have remembered that turning left would take him into the business district, where some of his and Marcie's favorite restaurants were.

But he didn't turn. He paused until the light turned green and then continued east. Unaware he had just finished his thirteenth mile of the night, more than he typically walked in a week.

Unaware that one of his sneakers had come partially untied. Unaware he was already in the first stage of dehydration.

And unaware a traffic camera in the stoplight had taken his picture.

Because he was *walking*.

Walking.

"Jim, I think we've got something on that missing person."

Officer Jim Gregg spun around in his chair. His partner, Eric Torrey, was holding his desk phone and waving him over.

"Go ahead," Torrey said. The person on the other line spoke for a minute, and then Torrey tapped something into the computer. An image came up, the kind of grainy picture that Gregg recognized as coming from a traffic cam. It was dark but not so much that he couldn't see the figure captured mid-stride. An adult male wearing a hooded New York Giants sweatshirt and sneakers.

Torrey jotted some notes on a scrap of paper. "Got it. Thanks." He hung up and turned to Gregg. "That was Nyack police. Someone reported a man walking on Route 9W heading out of town toward Piermont. They said he looked homeless and they almost hit him 'cause he was right on the edge of the road. The desk sergeant remembered our BOLO for Brenner and checked the traffic cams in town. They've got someone heading out there now."

"Fuckin' weird," Gregg said. "If that's him, he walked all the way from Rocky Point to Nyack? Why? It doesn't make sense."

Torrey shrugged. "People do crazy shit. Maybe he just had a breakdown. Better than eating a bullet."

"Yeah, I guess. Man, I feel sorry for that family."

Roger was *walking*, so he didn't notice the SUV pacing him on the road until an amplified voice called out.

"Sir. Please stop and identify yourself."

Roger looked at the vehicle. Black and white, with Nyack Police Department on the side. A man in a blue uniform was staring at him through the driver-side window.

Neither the words or the fact of it being the police touched the conscious part of Roger's brain, which had drifted into a deep stupor. But they did trigger a distant memory of the proper response.

He smiled and waved.

Walking.

The officer cursed and repeated the order to stop.

Walking.

Walking.

The SUV's engine revved up and it pulled ahead, then swerved onto the shoulder, blocking his way.

Roger went around it, nearly tripping and falling into the shallow ditch bordering the left side of the shoulder.

"Hey!" Doors slammed behind him. Footsteps thudded.

A hand grabbed his shoulder and spun him around.

"Mister, are you okay? What the hell?"

Roger found himself facing a tall, burly man. *A police officer.* Yes.

"Walking," he said.

"I see that. Are you Roger Brenner?"

Roger nodded and tried to move but the officer held him by the arms, forcing him to lift his feet while staying in place.

"What's your name, bud?" said a second voice. Another uniformed man joined the first.

"Name? Roger. Yes, Roger Brenner. I'm walking." Roger pushed against the other man's hands but they didn't give.

"Call it in."

The second man nodded and spoke into the radio mic on his shoulder.

"I'm walking," Roger said. "Please, let me go."

"Sorry, you're coming with us. You're family's worried sick about you."

"No. I'm walking." A piece of the old Roger woke up, responding to the new stimuli. "I haven't done anything wrong. I'm walking. That's not illegal."

The two cops looked at each other.

"He's right," the second one said, tapping his chest just below his body cam. "We can't just haul him back to the station 'cause his wife is upset. Guy could sue the shit out of the police. And us."

The first officer grimaced.

"I need to walk. I have a destination." Roger's stepping motions grew more agitated. *Walking.* He should be *walking.*

"Fine." The officer let go. Roger smiled and immediately started forward again.

Walking.

"What the fuck was that?" Officer Eric Grier watched Brenner stride away like nothing at all was wrong.

"I don't know. Drugs? Maybe he's kinda slow upstairs?" replied Officer Larry Wermont.

"The BOLO didn't say anything about the guy having mental problems. Maybe we should've brought him in."

"No thanks, I don't need that kinda trouble. We'll call it in and let Rocky Point take care of it. And in the meantime, we'll follow him. Make sure he's safe."

Grier shook his head.

"This is some weird shit. And it ain't even a full moon."

Driving down 9W in the back of the police car, Marcie Brenner tried to grasp the facts of the situation. None of it made sense. Roger taking off without a word. And then walking all the way to Nyack, where he wouldn't even stop for the police. All he'd said was that he wanted to keep walking.

It sounded unbelievable.

Had he suffered a stroke? Had a mental breakdown?

You'll know in a few minutes.

Officers Gregg and Torrey had shown up at the house to say Roger had been located. Now they were taking her to him, in the hope that she could talk to him, get him to come home. Since he'd done nothing wrong, the police couldn't do force him to go with them.

The road straightened out up ahead. They were almost into the town of Grand View-on-Hudson, already past the exit to the Tappan Zee Bridge. Up ahead, flashing red-and-blue lights showed where the Nyack Police SUV was still pacing Roger.

When the Rocky Point squad car pulled up, the driver of the other vehicle waved at them and drove away.

Officer Gregg pulled off the road ahead of Roger. The two officers exited the car and opened Marcie's door. She ran back to Roger and then had to jump aside or he would've walked right into her.

"Roger!" She trotted alongside him. "Roger! Stop. What are you doing?"

"Walking," he said, his voice as cheerful as if he were simply taking a stroll around the block.

"I can see that. Why? You just disappear without a word? We were worried sick. Roger, stop and talk to me!"

Marcie stepped in front of him and held out her hands.

Roger swerved around her and kept going.

"What the…?" She was left staring at the police car that was now almost twenty yards back, the two officers silhouettes in the glare of the headlights.

"No. No friggin' way." She turned and ran after him. This time, she grabbed him by the sweatshirt and hung on until he stopped. But even then, his feet kept moving as if he were marching in place.

Something is seriously wrong with my husband.

That thought chilled her more than discovering he was missing or the hours she'd spent wondering if he was dead.

"Roger. Do you know who I am? Can you

understand me?"

"Sure." He smiled, and beneath the crusted road grit he looked perfectly sane. Her Roger. "I'm Roger. You're my wife, Marcie. You found me. I'm fine. Now I have to keep walking."

"What? Why? Where the fuck are you going?" She didn't loosen her grip. The entire conversation felt like a dream. Or an acid trip.

"Walking." He jerked hard from side to side until pulled free from her grasp.

Without another word, he started down the road again.

This time, she was too stunned to chase after him. A few moments later, the police car rolled up.

"Couldn't help overhearing, ma'am," said Officer Gregg. "I think you need to go about this in a different way."

"A… what?" She watched her husband stroll down the road.

"Get in. Do you know a good doctor?"

Route 9W took Roger through the town of Piermont and into Sparkill. While crossing an intersection, he caught his left foot in a pothole, stumbled, and lost his sneaker.

He left it behind as he continued walking.

At just after three a.m., he crossed into New Jersey. Not long after, the road widened and despite the late hour, traffic picked up, thanks to his proximity to the George Washington Bridge and a major highway. His gait had become slightly erratic because he wore only the one sneaker. His left foot was scraped and bleeding where rocks and sand had already worn the bottom of his sock to threads. Blisters bulged on the heel and ball of his right foot, the thin insole of the sneaker not up to the challenge of so much force and movement.

The pain of his injuries registered dimly in the deepest part of Roger's consciousness, no different than his vague awareness of the temperature and color of the sky.

None of it slowed him down.

Walking. Walking.

Must walk.

All that mattered was forward motion. One foot and then the other. Keep going until…

Until it's time to stop.

Yes, that was it. He had known when to start, he would know when to stop. A part of him wished Marcie was there, so he could tell her. Then she wouldn't worry.

Nothing to worry about. He was fine.

He was *walking*.

Marcie sat at the kitchen table drinking coffee as dark and cold as the September night. The only light came from the digital clocks on the stove and microwave and the glow of her phone each time a message came in.

The police had dropped her off with the promise to update her every hour or so about Roger. And they'd kept their word. As much as she hated sitting there, doing abso-fucking-lutely nothing, they'd told her over and over it was all she could do until morning, when she and her doctor would be able to petition a judge for what Officer Gregg had called an involuntary mental health commitment order, or IMHC. Basically, the court would be putting her temporarily in charge of his physical and mental health due to the fact that he was a danger to himself. He'd be committed to a psychiatric facility for up to 48 hours of observation and a determination would be made regarding his mental status.

If the doctors decided he needed inpatient treatment, she would then remain responsible for him until such a time as they said he was okay. If that projected to be long-term, she could go back to the court and petition to be made his permanent guardian.

Conversely, if the doctors fixed whatever was wrong with him in a short time, then he'd simply return home and the IMHC would be cancelled.

She'd already spoken to Dr. Wilson Abrams, who'd been Roger and Marcie's physician for more than ten years. He'd agreed that something was very wrong and promised to provide the necessary documentation for the court in the morning.

In the meantime, there was nothing to do except wait and hope Roger wasn't hit by a car. The fact that the police were keeping tabs on him eased her anxiety a bit, but she still knew she wouldn't be getting any sleep that night. Instead, she'd brewed a pot of coffee, sent the kids to bed—after promising them their father would be safe and the doctors would soon be taking care of him—and parked herself in the kitchen.

What the hell, Roger? she kept thinking. He was obviously experiencing some kind of mental breakdown. She could accept that. Now fear was giving way to anger.

It wasn't fair. He'd stuck her with having to explain to their children that something was wrong with their father's brain, that he didn't abandon them, it was a disease, just like panic attacks, or gambling, or depression. That he just needed some help.

A mother shouldn't have to tell her kids those things.

Thanks a fucking lot, Roger.

She took another sip of coffee and wished she had a cigarette to go with it. She'd quit when she found out she was pregnant with Patty and never gone back to them. But now she craved one. They always eased her nerves.

What if he never gets better?

How would they survive if he was institutionalized for years, or forever? Her salary wouldn't be enough, even if they got permanent disability. They'd lose the house.

"Why, Roger? Why?"

Her only answer was the silence of the kitchen.

"Hello, Trish? This is Nick Larson, Rocky Point PD. You still paying for tips about stories? 'Cause I got a doozy for you."

Trish VanDerBot, the overnight news anchor for Channel 23, listened, her smile growing as her old high school classmate spoke. When he hung up, she immediately ran to her producer's office.

This one would be well worth the hundred bucks it had cost her.

"Mom, come quick!"

Marcie dropped the toast she'd been buttering and ran for the living room. Patty's voice had sounded panicked and—

Her daughter was pointing at the TV, her eyes wide. Next to her, Ben wore a similarly shocked expression.

"Dad's on the news."

Marcie shifted her attention to the screen as Patty turned up the volume.

"—identified as Roger Brenner, age forty-six, of Rocky Point. Brenner apparently left his house yesterday afternoon and was reported missing, only to turn up hours later several towns away from his home and family, walking down the highway."

The blonde news anchor's voice rose a half-octave, incredulity overcoming journalistic objectivity. Behind her was a picture of Roger. Marcie recognized it as his Facebook profile pic.

"We now go live to field correspondent Alice Kocera, who is with Roger Brenner right now in, believe it or not, Tenafly, New Jersey. Alice?"

The picture changed to a live feed, a close shot of a dark-haired woman in a puffy jacket walking briskly along the side of a four-lane road. In the distance, the first gray of dawn was lightening the horizon.

With the morning rush still more than an hour away, cars whizzed by in both directions. A few honked their horns when they noticed the news team. A young man leaned out his window and shouted "Bababooey!"

"Hello, this is Alice Kocera, and as you can see this isn't an ordinary morning for me. I'm on Route 9W in Tenafly, a busy and dangerous highway. And with me is Roger Brenner."

The camera pulled back to show a second figure. A man in jeans and a blue New York Giants sweatshirt. His clothes were filthy. Sometime during the night he'd lost both sneakers. All that remained of his socks were the parts covering his ankles. His feet were black with dirt and the bottoms covered in raw, torn flesh. Kocera increased her pace, allowing the camera to move up alongside Roger, showing his profile.

"Oh, my god," Marcie whispered.

The effects of his non-stop walk were already showing. He'd lost several pounds. You could see it in his face. His eyes were sunken and his cheeks flatter, the roundness of good living already disappearing. His morning stubble contained more gray than usual—or maybe that was just from the harsh glare of the camera light—making him appear ten years older. His eyes were bloodshot from exhaustion and road grit. His hair stuck out in all directions, giving him the appearance of a wild man.

But what struck Marcie the hardest was the contented smile he wore.

"Mr. Brenner, can you tell us why you're doing this?"

"Walking." Roger's voice was dry and raspy, but still clear.

"Yes, we can see that." Kocera glanced at the camera and you could read her thoughts as clearly as if she'd spoken them. *He's crazy.* "What made you decide to walk from New York to New Jersey?"

"Need to walk. Time to walk."

"I see." The reporter stumbled slightly, righted herself. She was starting to have trouble moving backwards and maintaining her balance at that speed. "What about your family, Mr. Brenner?

They're very worried about you."

Roger looked at the camera and his smile widened. "Love them. Kids. Marcie. Walking now."

Love them. Oh, Jesus. Roger, what the hell happened—

"Mr. Brenner, don't you think you should stop for a bit? Have something to drink? And a doctor really should look at your feet. You could—"

"Can't stop. Must walk. Walking."

Kocera came to a halt. Roger continued past her. She looked at the camera, a grave expression on her face.

"Well, there you have it. Roger Brenner is walking. When this strange journey will end, only he knows. All we can hope is that it ends safely. Reporting from Tenafly, this is Alice Kocera."

The picture switched back to the studio, where the blonde anchor shook her head slowly.

"Thank you, Alice. We all hope that. When we come back, we'll have special guest Chef Olaf Smitherson right here in the studio cooking his favorite snacks for the big game!"

"Turn it off," Marcie said, her voice rising. "Turn it off!"

Patty grabbed the remote and hit the Off button.

Seeing the alarmed looks on her children's faces, Marcie burst into tears. Before she could apologize, the phone rang.

"Mrs. Brenner? It's Doctor Abrams. Can you meet me at the courthouse at nine o'clock?"

Roger was *walking. Walking.* He no longer felt his feet or his legs; even the dim registration of pain was gone. His arms swung at his sides as much from the motion of his body as from actual muscular contractions. His lungs and heart pumped in sync with his stride, never increasing or decreasing, even when he went up or down steep hills.

The cuts on his feet no longer left bloody prints in his wake. Dirt and trash served as bandages.

Blisters had formed and popped on the insides of his thighs and in his armpits. The injured skin had sloughed away, leaving raw circles that oozed blood and clear fluids.

Even the roof of his mouth was irritated from his dry tongue rubbing against it. Dehydration had caused his gums to recede and pale, giving him an almost skeletal appearance when he smiled or spoke, something he did in time to his steps.

"Walking. Walking. Walking."

Police units from each town he passed through had taken turns driving behind or alongside him, both to track his progress and keep him safe from traffic. A few officers had tried talking to him. He'd either ignored them or interrupted his personal narration to give short, emotionless answers.

"I'm walking." "Must walk." "Can't stop. Walking."

Following Alice Kocera's exclusive, all the local news outlets had dispatched reporters to cover the bizarre story of the enigmatic Walking Man. Most of them stole the Stephen King book title for their stories (a few even referenced it), while others tried to gain extra viewers, readers, and social media hits by coming up with their own monikers. Long Distance Man. The Traveler. Walker-Man.

Roger paid no attention to the cars and vans trailing him. He responded when spoken to and then promptly forgot the conversations ever happened.

He only knew that he was *walking*.

Nothing else mattered.

It took the Honorable Ellen Kostas all of ten minutes to sign the involuntary mental health commitment order. Based on Dr. Abrams' assessment, the news clips of Roger, and Marcie's description of her interaction with him on the road, she issued her decision without even needing time to mull it over.

Armed with the paperwork and a reservation at Rocky Point Psychiatric Hospital, Marcie and Dr. Abrams drove to Fort Lee, New Jersey, accompanied by Officers Gregg and Torrey, who'd been assigned as their police liaisons. They would bring Roger to the hospital, whether he agreed or not.

Thanks to Channel 21 breaking the story of Roger's antics, neither Ben nor Patty had wanted to go to school. And Marcie readily agreed; being in the presence of obnoxious, rude, and uncaring teenagers was the last thing they needed. But she couldn't bring them with her. Even if the cops had allowed it, there was no way she wanted them to see their father up close, not in his current state. They'd be scarred for life.

And although she had no problem leaving Patty to watch Ben for a few hours, this wasn't a good time for them to be alone. So she'd called Anne Voit from down the street. Anne didn't work and she'd been more than willing to spend the day at their house and make sure the kids did anything but watch the news.

Of course, they'd probably just be on social media the whole time, but there was nothing she could do to prevent that except take their phones and laptops away. And they'd already been punished enough by their father's irrational behavior.

Even though the officers had warned her that the public had grown more aware of Roger and his singular travels, she hadn't been prepared for what they encountered when they arrived.

An entire media circus rolled behind him like a modern-day wagon train.

Oblivious to the police car and the six television vans behind it, he was still walking down the shoulder of 9W. Despite his ruined feet and obvious physical unhealth, he maintained a steady, purposeful stride.

"What the actual fuck?" Marcie hit the brake too

hard, causing the car to jerk and throwing Dr. Abrams forward. She eased up on the pedal and peered through the windshield, trying to see around the line of vehicles. Ahead of her, their police escort flipped on his lights and moved into the other lane. Marcie followed, staying close as the cruiser passed the media vultures and caught up to the New Jersey State Police car coasting along just behind Roger.

The trooper flashed its lights and gave a single whoop of its siren, and then sped up and headed down the road. Officer Gregg steered the cruiser over and then moved ahead before easing onto the shoulder to block Roger's path. Marcie pulled in at the edge of the shoulder as the two officers got out.

"Roger Brenner." Gregg held up the signed papers. "We have a court approved order remanding you into our custody. We will be taking you to a hospital for evaluation."

Roger kept walking. When he got within ten feet of the officers, he tried shifting to his left to go around them but a waist-high concrete guard wall prevented any detour. When he realized he couldn't go to the sides or forward, he settled into the same weird stepping in place motion that he'd done the last time Marcie spoke to him.

"Walking," he said, his voice hoarser than when she'd heard him on TV. "Need to keep walking."

"Roger." Marcie stood in front of him, Abrams by her side. "Roger, do you understand what we're doing? You're not well. We're taking you to the hospital."

"No, need to walk. Walking. Nothing wrong. Fine. Walking."

"He's out of it." Officer Torrey strode forward. "Doc, I think you should give him something. We don't want him struggling when we put him in the car. He might get hurt."

"Yes, of course." Abrams had told Marcie earlier it might come to this. He had a sedative injection ready. It wouldn't knock Roger out, but he'd be pretty much limp as a noodle for a few hours. Long enough to get him back to Rocky Point Psych.

Abrams returned to the car and brought out a small black satchel. He rummaged inside it and removed a syringe and a small glass vial. He stuck the syringe in, withdrew the contents, and tapped the syringe a couple of times. Tranquilizer in hand, he approached Marcie and the officers, who were still surrounding the walking-in-place Roger.

"You'll need to hold him so I can make the injection safely," Adams told Gregg and Torrey.

"Got it."

The officers moved forward and took Roger by the arms. He instantly grew agitated, trying to shake loose while at the same time continuing his stepping motions.

"Let go. Need to walk. Not right. Must walk."

With his free hand, Adams lifted Roger's sweatshirt and t-shirt, exposing the upper part of Roger's buttocks.

"Hold it right there! Don't you dare give that man anything unless you wanna be charged with assault and kidnapping."

The loud, Brooklyn-filled voice caused everyone except Roger to turn. Approaching them was a portly, middle-aged man in a dark suit. He held a piece of paper in one hand. Behind him was a New York State Police officer.

"Who the hell are you?" Marcie asked.

"Benjamin P. Thoma, Attorney. And this," he waved the paper, "is an injunction against the involuntary commitment order Mrs. Brenner has so surreptitiously obtained."

"Surreptitiously? There was nothing—"

"No excuses. I am representing Mr. Brenner and his right to remain free."

"Mr. Brenner is obviously in no state to make any decisions," Gregg said, his voice tinged with annoyance.

"Well, let's see about that." Thoma moved past Marcie and stood face-to-face with Roger. "Mr. Brenner, what is it you would like to do?"

"Walk. Must walk." said Roger.

"Uh-huh. Would you rather go home?"

"No home. Walk. Keep walking."

Thoma glanced at Marcie and Adams, one eyebrow cocked up.

"Mr. Brenner, do you understand what we are saying?"

"Yes. I want to walk. Not go home."

"Are you incapacitated in any way?"

"No. Fine. Fine. Need to walk."

Thoma looked at Marcie and then the officers.

"He sounds pretty rational to me."

"Bullshit!" Marcie shouted. "He's half dead and talking like he had a stroke. His feet look like someone took a cheese grater to them. He's filthy. He hasn't eaten or slept or had anything to drink. For fuck's sake, he shit himself!"

"None of that means he's crazy. Marathon runners soil themselves. They keep running with blisters on their feet. They don't eat or drink until the race is over."

"This isn't a race," Adams said. "This man decided out of nowhere to just walk, and not stop. He's obviously in a mental fugue of some kind. He needs professional help."

"Would you say the same thing to David Cruz?" Thoma asked.

Marcie frowned. "What? Who the hell is that?"

"David Cruz. He walked from New York to Florida. He was writing music at the dinner table when he suddenly felt it was time to go to Florida. Four hours later, he was on his way. Said it was a walk of faith, to spread the word of God. Eventually he wants to try walking across every country in the world."

"That, that's nothing like this," Torrey said.

"How do you know? Have you asked him?" Thoma turned back to Roger. "Mr. Brenner, do you have a reason for walking?"

"Yes." Roger nodded his head. "I have to walk. Need to walk. There is a reason. Important. Everyone will know."

"Uh-huh. Mr. Brenner, would you like me to make sure no one stops you from walking?"

Roger gave another nod, and smiled. "Yes. Need to walk. Must walk. Walking."

Thoma slapped the letter against Gregg's chest. "Until further notice, no one may lay a hand on my client. From what I have seen, he's of sound mind. And the fact that he can do what, twenty-five miles, thirty miles, without stopping? Without even taking a break? That shows me he's of sounder body than any of us."

"Son of a bitch." Gregg read the court order, started to crumple it in his hands, and then stopped himself. "This is legal. Doc, put the needle away."

"No!" Marcie stepped toward Gregg but stopped when he held his hand out. "We've got a court order, too. Doesn't ours have priority or something? My husband is dying here!"

"I'm sorry, Mrs. Brenner. In cases like this our hands are tied. It's up to a judge to decide which one takes precedence. You go back to the courthouse to get this straightened out. We'll keep an eye on your husband. I promise, we won't let anything happen to him. And just so you know," Gregg directed the rest of his words right at Thoma. "The law also states that if Mr. Brenner's life is in imminent danger, or he commits a crime, or he is injured or loses consciousness, we can act in his best interests, just like we would with any citizen."

"Understood," Thoma said. He turned to Marcie and gave her a quick two-fingered salute. "Good day, Mrs. Brenner. I guess I'll see you in court. I suggest you hire an attorney."

The squat man waddled off to his car, leaving Marcie struggling not to shout every filthy insult she knew at his back.

"C'mon, Marcie, we should do what he says." Doctor Adams took her gently by the elbow.

"And Mrs. Brenner?"

She looked back at Officer Torrey, who pointed past her down the road, where the line of media vans had all pulled over and apparently recorded the entire scene.

"I think you better get the best damn attorney you can find."

Finding an attorney and arranging an emergency appearance before a judge took two days. In that time, Roger walked forty-eight miles, reaching the shore town of Tom's River, New Jersey, just after nine a.m.

By then, he had become national news.

All the New York, New Jersey, and even Philadelphia outlets, print and electronic, had crews covering him twenty-four hours a day. And the national stations and wire services were providing twice-a-day updates on his condition and location.

Graphics detailing his trek were shown side-by-side with detailed pictures and videos of his rapidly deteriorating condition. He'd lost so much weight that his pants were riding low on his hips like a teenager. He swam inside his sweatshirt, which was now covered in layers upon layers of dust and dirt, to the point where you couldn't even tell the original color of blue. His face was so drawn and pale he appeared more skeleton than man. Crust surrounded his eyes, which had taken on a distinctly yellowish hue. Brown stains covered the back of his pants and down his legs from the times he'd voided his bowels.

But the worst were the shots of his feet.

Each time he lifted one to step forward, the horrific damage was visible to the cameras. His skin was completely abraded away, exposing muscle, connective tissue, and in some places glimpses of bone. Gravel and bits of litter were embedded in the raw, inflamed meat.

Of course, the cameras made sure to focus on every grotesque detail.

And still he walked on, maintaining a steady pace of two miles an hour.

Each news show had their own medical professionals commenting on his physical and mental status. Newspapers quoted experts on everything from anatomy to schizophrenia in an attempt to fill space and increase clicks.

With nothing to do but wait, Marcie was forced to follow Roger's progress through the TV and internet. She couldn't leave town to be with Roger because she had to remain close by for when she received word the judge would hear her plea. In the meantime, she and her children were getting inundated with calls and messages from people wanting interviews, offering help, or simply being nosy.

On several occasions she'd been ready to just drive to Jersey, throw Roger in the car, and take him to the hospital. Let the lawyers fight it out while her husband received the help he so desperately needed. But her new attorney, Alan Koy, had warned her that was the last thing she should do.

"You could end up in jail yourself, and then you'd be no help at all to Roger or your children."

Not that I'm much help sitting on my ass in the living room. When she'd finally gotten the call from Koy that they had a meeting set in two hours, she nearly screamed with relief.

A shower did little to erase the dark smudges of exhaustion from under her eyes or the stress lines from her forehead and around her mouth. She thought about going heavy with her makeup but then decided she'd rather the judge get a look at just how frantic with worry she was.

She'd have preferred to leave Ben and Patty at home, but Koy had said it was important for the judge to see them, too.

"A reminder that Roger has a family that needs him, that this case is about more than one man's right to self-destruct."

Neither Ben nor Patty spoke on the ride to the county courthouse. They'd both been mostly uncommunicative since Marcie returned home without their father.

"You promised," Patty had said, her voice dripping with reproach as she held up her pad. On it was a picture of Roger's bloody, ruined feet. "That doesn't look safe to me."

Then she'd stormed off to her room and slammed the door.

Now they sat in the row behind Marcie. She'd glanced back a couple of times. Patty was wringing her hands and Ben was staring blankly at the empty judge's bench. He'd heard the statements from Koy and Benjamin Thoma. Both of them had presented video and photographic evidence to back up their statements. Then the judge told them he would consider everything in the privacy of his chambers and they would reconvene in a half hour.

Now, thirty-seven minutes later, Marcie was doing all she could not to fidget in her seat. Next to her, Koy had a sheet of paper covered in handwritten notes that he kept reading and re-reading. Which did nothing to ease her nerves because it made her think he was reviewing things he'd forgotten to say.

Across the aisle, Thoma sat with his hands folded on the table, wearing a smug look Marcie wanted to slap off his face.

Tick-tick-tick-tick-tick.

Marcie looked around, wondering where the muted clicking sound was coming from. Koy leaned over and placed his hand over hers. The sound stopped and she realized she'd been tapping her nails on the table.

"How much longer—"

The door to Judge Meriweather's chambers opened, cutting her off in mid-sentence. Koy motioned for her to stand as Meriweather took his seat behind the bench.

"Be seated." When everyone did, Meriweather cleared his throat and looked right at Koy and Marcie.

"Mrs. Brenner. I have thought very hard about this. And, to be honest, my first inclination was to decide in your favor. And then I saw this." He motioned to a young man in a brown suit, who wheeled a television on a metal rack to a spot between the bench and the two attorney tables. The man pressed a button on a remote and the screen came on.

"This happened to be on the news in my office while I was reviewing all the information. And while I normally wouldn't consider outside evidence, I believe this is pertinent to this case. Sam?"

The man nodded and touched the remote again.

A recording came on. Roger Brenner, walking down the road. Marcie gasped and behind her, Patty whimpered.

He looked even worse than he had two hours earlier. If not for the modern buildings behind him and the cars driving past, he could easily have been mistaken for a cancer victim, or a prisoner of war, someone hanging on to life by a thread.

And yet, his tragically gaunt face still held an expression of contentment.

"This is Susan Marsh reporting from Bayville, New Jersey, where Roger Brenner, the Walker as he's now being called, has just reached the one hundred and thirteen mile mark of his enigmatic journey. And now, the most amazing thing is happening."

The camera pulled back to show more than a dozen people behind Roger. All of them wore the same serene expression. Some were dressed for walking, with sneakers, jeans, and sweatshirts. Others looked like they'd just stopped whatever they'd been doing and left their houses. Marcie saw sweats, t-shirts, flip-flops, and one zombie-eyed housewife in a robe and slippers.

"As you can see, Roger Brenner is starting to accumulate followers." The reporter, a dark-haired woman in her forties, moved right up next to Roger. "Mister Brenner, can you tell us what this is all about? Do you have a destination in mind?"

"Walking," Roger said, never pausing. "The

destination is the end. The end is the destination. Everyone has a path. I follow mine."

"So, you're saying there is a purpose to this, this journey of yours?"

"Everything has a purpose. I see mine. Destination. Walking."

"Well, now," Susan Marsh uttered a quick laugh, more of a practiced twitter. "That's very profound. What do you say to the people who are calling you, er, irrational? Who think you've had some sort of breakdown?"

"Breakdown. Epiphany. Comprehension. All words. We are walking. Walking."

"Well, there you have it. This is Susan Marsh, live with Roger Brenner, the Walker."

Meriweather's assistant shut the TV off and wheeled it away. Meriweather steepled his fingers under his chin and took a deep breath before speaking.

"As much as it pains me to say it, that is a man who sounds completely rational. Wait," he said, holding up a hand when Koy made to rise from his chair. "His actions are... unusual. Extreme. Definitely eccentric. But based on what I saw and heard, it is my judgement that Roger Brenner is no more a candidate for involuntary commitment than anyone who decides to go on a religious pilgrimage or fast for a month in order to cleanse their mind and body."

"What?" Marcie jumped up and Koy bounded to

his feet beside her.

"Your honor! How can you say that? The man is clearly a danger to himself. He's beyond dehydrated and his feet are going to require major surgery. That's if he doesn't lose them altogether."

Behind them, Patty burst into tears and Benny got up and ran out of the room.

"That's probably all true, Counselor," Meriweather said, nonplussed by the attorney's outburst. "But there is a difference between committing an act of self-harm, such as slicing your wrists with a razor or taking a bottle of pills, and ignoring your own safety in order to follow your beliefs or aspirations. If the latter were a committable offense, we'd have to lock away every religious snake-handler, every scientist who risks their life working with radiation or deadly viruses, hell, every one of those contestants on talent shows who hit themselves with hammers or eat light bulbs."

Koy started to say something else but Meriweather raised his voice and drowned him out.

"I'm sorry, but until Mr. Brenner does something purposeful to injure himself or someone else, or he loses the ability to speak coherently, I am declaring him sane and competent."

"Thank you, your honor." Benjamin Thoma picked up his briefcase, gave a jaunty salute to Marcie, and headed for the doors.

Marcie looked at Koy.

"Now what?"

The attorney shrugged.

"Now we hope he either passes out or comes to his senses. I'll file a motion for appeal, but that will take days."

"My husband doesn't have days," Marcie said.

"Then I suggest you go talk to him again."

Walking.

One step. Another. Another.

Walking.

It was so simple now. Roger was starting to see it all so clearly. The path before him, his purpose. The reason he'd been chosen.

Not everything. Not yet. Bits and pieces, like seeing all the fragments of a puzzle someone had dumped on a table, but there was no box to go with it. No way to know what the final picture would be. Only glimpses of possibilities, a leaf here, a stone there, a section of sky, half a cloud.

But his path shined brightly ahead of him, green as fresh-mown grass, green as emeralds, glowing bright as neon. All he had to do was keep walking.

He no longer felt his body or the world around him. There was no cold, no warm. No pain, no pleasure. The world simply *was*. *He* was. He knew the solidity of the ground beneath his feet, the rush of wind when vehicles went by. He felt the pressure of touch when he brushed against a tree or light post as he passed.

He understood the words of the people who came to visit him, but he quickly forgot them. Words didn't matter.

Walking mattered.

The destination mattered.

The purpose mattered.

"Walking," he whispered.

Behind him, thirty-three people repeated it.

"Walking."

Waretown sits right between Ocean Township and Barnegat Beach. More a village than a town, it's the kind of place you can miss if you blink while driving through it. Located only a few blocks from the ocean, the center of town only exists to service tourists heading to the larger vacation spots like Long Beach Island and Barnegat. Over the years, Waretown has seen its share of hurricanes, tropical storms, and nor'easters.

It was not prepared for the tempest that was Roger Brenner and the Walkers.

By the time Marcie got there, the streets were so crowded she had to park in a supermarket and walk back a block, Patty and Ben in her wake, to meet up with Roger.

Roger's followers had grown in number in the two hours since Marcie stormed out of the courthouse and took her attorney's advice.

Stretched out behind him two and three abreast, they resembled a miniature parade with Roger leading the way.

Bringing up the rear were at least ten media vans, some riding the shoulder, others causing traffic delays because they coasted along at the same pace as the walkers.

Waretown police were parked at the entrance to town, vehicle lights flashing, providing warnings to approaching traffic. Hastily arranged detours routed cars and delivery trucks down side streets, creating havoc for locals trying to go to work or run their errands.

As prepared as she thought she was by how Roger had looked on the video, Marcie couldn't hold back fresh tears when she came face to face with the thing that used to be her husband.

Up close, in real life, he could've passed for a reanimated corpse like the ones in Ben's favorite horror movies.

He'd lost patches of his hair. His eyes were so sunken and discolored she couldn't even tell what they once looked like. His cadaverous face was almost unrecognizable, his lips pulled back to reveal pale gums already beginning to recede from his teeth. There was almost no fat left on his body, which was blatantly eating away at itself to keep him moving. The tendons of his neck stood out like cables under his skin and the bones of his hands were so clear you could count them.

When she reached a point only a couple of yards away, the stench rolling off his body hit her like an invisible fist. Shit, piss, and a sweet, rotten odor like meat left out on counter for too long in the summer.

"Oh, Roger," she said, falling in step next to him. "Please, for the love of God, stop this and come home. Your family needs you."

"Dad, please," Patty echoed. She was crying now, too. Ben said nothing; he kept his gaze anywhere but on his father.

"Walking," Roger said, eyes facing forward. He no longer blinked. When he spoke, his tongue, so dry it had paled to almost white and had yellow fuzz growing on it, stuck to the roof of his mouth and made a smacking noise when it dislodged. The overpowering foulness of his breath made her gag.

"Enough with the walking!" she shouted. "This is crazy! Stop and come home, goddammit!"

"Can't. Important. We have a purpose. Seen it. Everyone will see. Must keep walking."

"More important than me? Than your kids? Your life?"

When Roger didn't answer, the last atom of her self-control exploded. With a wordless scream she lunged at him, battering his chest and arms with her fists. She kicked his leg. He stumbled but kept walking.

"Enough! This ends now!" She hit him again and now someone was shouting at her to stop, to leave daddy alone, but the words were distant, meaningless. All that mattered was putting an end to Roger's stupid quest or search for enlightenment before he died in the middle of a New Jersey road.

Strong hands grabbed her and pulled her away. She fought them, twisting from side to side.

"Let me go! I have to stop him. He's my husband!"

"That's enough," a deep male voice said. The hands turned her around and she found herself staring at two police officers.

"No! He needs to come home. He needs help!" She managed to pull one arm free and tried to lunge at Roger again. But he'd already moved several feet ahead and instead she knocked one of the other walkers off-balance. He bumped hard into an older woman who fell and then got up again without a sound. Blood oozing from her scraped knees, she resumed her steady pace while murmuring "Walking, walking."

"Hey!" one of the cops shouted. "Calm down, lady."

"Fuck you!" Marcie screamed. She lashed out with her foot, catching the officer in the shin. "I have to stop him before it's too late!"

"That's it," the other cop said. "You're under arrest. Let's go."

"No! Stop! Leave me the fuck alone! Let me go!" Marcie kicked out again, unable to do much with her arms. The cops' hands tightened with bruising force and they dragged her away from the eerie procession.

"Help! Help!" she shouted. A blue-clad arm appeared before her and she clamped her teeth on it. The officer cried out. The hands holding her let go and for one moment she was free. She had time to take a single step toward Roger.

Then her whole body exploded in pain and the world went dark.

"Marcie Brenner." An officer appeared at the cell bars, her dirty-blonde hair pulled back in a bun and a cold, angry look on her face. "You're bail's been paid. Let's go."

Marcie jumped up from her cot and hurried to the door as the officer opened it. She understood the cop's poorly hidden anger. The past twenty-four hours had provided plenty of time to contemplate the charges against her. Attacking a citizen. Resisting arrest. Assaulting an officer. It was that last one that had kept her locked up since the previous day. She'd been tasered, shoved into a police car, and dumped in a cell. Forced to wait three hours before she got her phone call. Suffered the indignity of getting fingerprinted and mug shots taken while still wearing the same pants she'd pissed after she basically got electrocuted.

Then she'd had to share the drunk tank with a homeless old lady and a giant of a woman who looked like she could lift a car, until Alan Koy showed up to negotiate her release. Only by then, the judges had all gone home for the day and she was told she'd have to remain in custody until her bail hearing the following day.

"Nothing I can do," Koy said, before he left her for the night.

"What about Patty and Ben?" They'd been her biggest worry. When she woke in her cell, the police had no idea of their whereabouts. They'd allowed her to check her phone, and she'd seen a message from Patty that they'd taken an Uber back to Rocky Point and were at a friend's house.

That message was the only thing that prevented the police from adding child endangerment to her list of crimes.

"They're fine," Koy had informed her. "I called Patty and your neighbor is there."

After he left, promising to meet her at the courthouse the next day, she was moved to a private cell not much larger than her bathroom at home. She'd done her best to clean up with water and toilet paper and then she'd sat on the thin mattress and cried until a guard brought dinner at six o'clock. A greasy hamburger and cold French fries with a can of cola, none of which helped the burning in her stomach.

Then there'd been nothing to do until lights out at ten p.m.

Sleep had taken a long time to arrive. Between thinking about Roger, her legal troubles, and the possibility of lice in the blankets, her mind refused to shut down.

When it finally did, images of shambling zombies filled her dreams and she woke up several times during the night shaking.

Breakfast was soggy buttered toast and fake scrambled eggs with lukewarm coffee. When the guard came to pick up the tray, he told Marcie her bail hearing was set for one p.m.

"Why so late?" she'd asked. His only answer was a sneer before he walked away.

She was further embarrassed at the hearing when reporters bombarded her with questions as she entered the courthouse. Still wearing her soiled clothes, unshowered, and without the benefit of makeup or a brush, she tried to hide her face as cameras surrounded her.

Twenty minutes later, she exited the building in disgrace. None of the charges had been dropped and bail set for ten thousand dollars.

"I'll take care of it," Koy said. "And then you can pay me back when you get home. You'll be out in an hour."

The hour had turned into two, but now she was finally free. After signing for her purse and keys, she went into the lobby, where Koy was waiting for her.

"I know you can't wait to get home, but we still have one more thing to take care of. The police towed your car. It's at the impound lot."

"Of course." Marcie was tempted to just leave it

there; she had to be back in two weeks for her court date. She could just drive Roger's car in the meantime. But it would mean some hefty fines adding up, and the way her legal fees were escalating, she'd need every penny in the bank.

Sure enough, it cost half a car payment for them to release the car. Koy walked her to it. As she went to open the door, he put out a hand, stopping her.

"Marcie. I know you're going to be tempted to drive back to Roger. Maybe you'll tell yourself it's just to see him. Just to make sure he's still alive. But then you'll stop. You'll want to get closer. To talk with him. Reason with him. Take my advice. Don't do it. Just get in your car and go home. The police will be looking for you and if you get arrested again, there won't be bail. You'll sit in that cell until your court date."

Marcie bit her lip. It was like he'd read her mind. She'd been planning on doing exactly that. Just driving past. Maybe slow down.

Really? That's it? You know damn well you'd stop, get out. And if you did that, if you got within shouting distance of him again… you'd lose it. Probably worse than before. Even now she could feel the rage, the frustration, simmering inside, ready to boil over in an instant.

"Marcie, please. As your attorney, I'm advising you. Go home to your children. Be there for them, they need you, their mother. I'm doing everything I can for Roger. So is Doctor Abrams. This fight isn't over. But when it is, not only will you have Roger in the hospital where he belongs, but you'll have a lawsuit like no one has ever seen. We'll sue the police, the county, and anyone else who prevented Roger from getting the care he needs."

"Jesus, I hope you're right." Marcie took a deep breath. Home. Sleep. Food. Then she could start planning out the next steps. Like how to pay the bills with Roger not working.

For the love of God, Roger. Why the hell couldn't you just have a midlife crisis like other husbands? Buy a Mustang. Fuck your secretary. Fuck all the secretaries! Anything but become a modern-day maharishi on a goddamn journey of enlightenment.

"Thanks, Alan," she said, and she meant it. The fury still burned inside her, but she had the lid back on the pot. For now, at least. He nodded and stepped away from the car. As she drove out, she saw him still watching her, probably waiting to see which direction she turned.

At the exit, she paused only for a second and then went left.

Toward home.

"In the latest Walker news, Roger Brenner now has more than two hundred followers. More and more people are joining what some are calling a mystical, and others a supernatural, congregation with each town he passes through. Like Brenner, these new Walkers seem oblivious to the world around them unless forced to speak. They do not stop to eat or drink, will not even acknowledge food if it's offered to them. They seem to have no control over bodily functions and no sense of pain. In Little Egg Harbor, police had to disperse a group of protesters who…"

"Residents of the sleepy seaside town of Mystic Village, New Jersey, woke this morning to a very unusual sight: More than two-hundred and fifty people walking down the main drag in what seemed to be a state of self-hypnosis. They are, of course, the Walkers, led by Roger Brenner of New York. They appear almost zombie-like as they march from one town to the next. Scientists are baffled by this astounding occurrence, and religious groups have begun comparing it to the story of the exodus of the Israelites from Egypt in the Bible…"

"In Smithville today, the Walker procession was greeted by a group of local religious leaders. Priests, rabbis, pastors, an imam, plus a woman claiming to be a witch and representing the Order of the Golden Light, met the Walkers at the edge of town to bless them with Holy Water, incense, and prayer. More than five hundred strong, the cavalcade continued by without so much as a pause. Father Ben Robb spoke to us after and said…"

"As the horde approaches Absecon, a suburb of

Atlantic City, it is hard to put into words what I'm seeing. Warning, the video we'll be showing depicts graphic damage and mutilation of human bodies. Roger Brenner, still at the front of the pack, which is now well over five hundred people, should by all rights be dead. There is no flesh on his feet; there is literally nothing but bone below his ankles and yet he is able to walk. His face is like something from a horror movie, the lips pulled back to reveal his teeth, his eyes sunken so far they look like black holes. Several of his earliest disciples are in a similar condition, although not as advanced. Most of the throng show signs of serious foot injuries, dehydration, and starvation. The smell emanating from the group is abhorrent, it reeks of disease and rot. More frightening than any of this, though, are the voices. All of them murmuring as one, almost like chanting in a temple. Walking, walking, walking. The same word, over and over. Honestly, Becca, I would rather be anywhere than—"

"Hello, Monica? Well, we seem to have lost audio and… what's that? I'm getting a report from Dan Noyes, our camera man…no, that can't be possible. That… oh, God. Is it really true? I've received distressing news. It appears our field reporter, Monica Hong, is has joined the crowd of Walkers."

Camera cuts to the group and zooms in on a middle-aged woman in a blue pantsuit. She is still holding her portable microphone in one hand and is walking in step with the others, her blank-eyed gaze straight forward. Her lips are moving in time with the people surrounding her. The words are soft but clear, like gentle waves rolling onto a beach.

"Walking. Walking. Walking."

In the three days following her arrest and release, Marcie focused on putting her life back together, or at the least the parts of it she could control.

Following Alan Koy's advice, she went home and did something she should've done days earlier: have a heart-to-heart conversation with Ben and Patty. She apologized over and over for losing her cool and leaving them alone in a strange town. She told them how she felt about what Roger had done, was doing. Admitted she wasn't just frightened, she was hurt. Angry. Confused. And to her surprise—and joy—they opened up to her about their feelings as well. The three of them cried and hugged on the couch and when their sobs eased up, she informed them that they couldn't keep sitting around in limbo.

"You're not making us go to school, are you?" Patty asked, a stricken look on her face. Seeing it, Marcie felt that fury, now bordering on hatred, toward Roger again. He'd done irreparable damage to his children and left her to fix things.

"No." She'd thought about it and come up with a solution. "I'm going to call your principals today and speak to them about you going one-hundred percent remote until this whole shit-show is over. If he won't agree, then I'll arrange for home schooling. I get that school wouldn't be a positive environment right now, but I can't let you fall behind in your studies, either."

Marcie then laid out her own plans. There was really nothing she could personally do for Roger at this point. Alan Koy was taking care of all the legal work. Trying to get the declaration of mental competence overturned. Negotiating with the court in Jersey to drop her charges due to extenuating circumstances. Attempting to get permission for a doctor to examine Roger *in situ*.

"If we have proof from a medical authority that Roger is in imminent danger, it will give us the leverage we need to have him declared *non compos mentis*."

"He's literally lost his feet. He looks minutes from death. That's not enough?" Marcie had gripped her phone so hard the edges cut into her hand. *Control. Keep control. For the kids.*

"Roger has pretty much stumped the medical community. More than a few big-name doctors already believe that Roger and some of the others are technically dead. And that's got our judge, and probably anyone else we appear before, in a bind. Most judges hate making decisions in high-profile, controversial cases. Especially instances that have never existed before. We need to get before one who wants the spotlight, wants to make a name for themself. I'm working on that, too."

With no ability to help Roger, Marcie was left with attending to her own needs. She took a long overdue shower. Put on makeup. Got online and reviewed the bank accounts. If she moved some money out of savings, they'd be able to pay the bills and buy groceries for at least four months. After that, it would mean dipping into the special accounts they had for vacations and emergencies.

This sure as hell qualifies as an emergency.

She didn't know what she'd do about legal fees. She'd had to quit her job, and Roger's company had fired him over a week ago. Another thing Koy said they'd handle later. The attorney had told her not to worry about his bill, they'd figure out a payment plan later. But if the figure was as large as she feared, it'd mean cashing in some of their retirement investments.

Then it was out to buy groceries. The refrigerator was cavernously empty.

That'll be another three hundred bucks at least, she thought with a grimace. Nothing like being unemployed and incomeless while the price of everything kept rising.

It was astounding to think that in less than two weeks she could go from contemplating a winter vacation in Colorado to wondering if she'd still have house by the end of the year.

Thanks a fucking lot, Roger.

As she started the car, she had a sudden feeling that the house wasn't the only thing she was in danger of losing.

Even if her husband survived, her marriage most likely wouldn't.

"Hi! Today on Top of the Morning, we have a special guest, Doctor Navi Ghosh, a preeminent professor of physiology and anatomy at Princeton University. Welcome, Dr. Ghosh."

"Very good to be here, Callie. Thank you."

"Dr. Ghosh, before we get to the reason you're here, which is to talk about the Walker phenomenon, can you tell us a little bit about yourself and the field you study?"

"Of course. I am the Chairman of the Physiology Department at Princeton. Physiology is the study of normal functions within living creatures. It covers a range of topics, including organs, anatomy, biological compounds, exercise and motion, everything from individual cells to muscular and nervous systems. It is, you could say, the study of how the body works."

"So, it would be safe to say you're something of an expert on the human body."

"Oh, yes, quite."

"And you're familiar with Roger Brenner and the other Walkers?"

"Yes, yes, very familiar. I spent a good portion of

the day yesterday examining them. In the wild, you could say."

"Great! Why don't you tell our audience what your, I guess as a scientist you'd say, hypothesis is?"

"The Walkers are quite an interesting phenomenon, Callie, as I'm sure you're aware. And I must say, they present quite a conundrum to those of us who study the biological sciences."

"How so?"

"Well, for starters, it should be physiologically impossible for Roger Brenner to still be alive, let alone performing constant physical activity. As numerous videos have shown, his body has deteriorated to the point of collapse. He is severely dehydrated and malnourished. The human body can only go a few days without water. Up to several weeks without food, yes, but water is essential for life. In the absence of those things, it starts to break down its own cells, which is what Roger Brenner has been doing for weeks now. He is literally eating himself. Beneath his clothes, there is almost no muscle or fat left, just skin stretched over bone. The flesh of his feet has rotted away, decomposed, fallen off. Yet the decay seems to have slowed almost to a stop above his ankles. Walking on bones is impossible; he should bleed out, fall over. His eyes have basically deflated, the liquid in them gone. His tongue is little more than a shriveled, blackened stump. His fingernails have fallen off and the tips of his phalanxes, the finger bones, can be seen poking through."

"My goodness! What you're describing sounds like something from a horror movie, or *The Walking Dead*."

"That is more accurate than you might think. What I'm describing is a man who should be dead. Yet he lives, breathes, and moves. What we are seeing with Roger Brenner, and the other Walkers who are also in various stages of deterioration, is something new and unheard of in modern science. The closest thing would be the Japanese monks who practiced *sokushinbutsu*, the art of self-mummification. Those monks would slowly starve themselves for years, ingesting just a few nuts and berries and tiny sips of water. Eventually, they took a special poison to preserve their flesh right before they finally succumbed to starvation. However, those monks did not walk several miles a day, nor did their flesh putrify while they were alive. What is happening with the Walkers is completely unique. They are quite literally transforming into living corpses."

"Wow! That amazing. And terrifying. Tell me, Doctor Ghosh, how do you explain why Brenner is doing this, and why so many people are following him now? I mean, at last count, he had almost fifteen hundred disciples."

"Callie, I have no explanation for that at all. I have spoken to several colleagues about this. Some of their theories are mass self-hypnosis, latent mental illness, or perhaps something biological."

"Biological? You mean, like a bio-weapon? Something in the water?"

"No. Well, probably not. A bio-weapon would affect more people. But something in Roger Brenner himself? That is possible. A virus he spreads, or even an aerosolized chemical compound. Or a fungal infection. However, I have trouble believing that is the cause. While it's true that some people who've had direct contact with the Walkers suddenly join them, others of the followers have come from miles away without any previous contact. It appears to be totally random."

"There's talk of the government putting an end to the whole affair. It's disrupting traffic, causing safety issues, and becoming a volatile trigger point for confrontations, not only among local citizens but also religious groups. Any thoughts on how we should be handling this?"

"I'm a scientist, not a law maker. But if anyone were to ask my opinion, I would say we need to study this singularly unique event in human history. Both to understand it, and to prevent it from happening again."

"Again? You don't think this is an isolated incident?"

"In science, there are no isolated incidents. Only first incidents."

"We have a court date set."

"Oh, thank God." Marcie closed her eyes. Three days of waiting, texting Koy every few hours only to be told there was no news yet, had worn her down. Even getting out of bed was a struggle now, and she spent most of her waking hours in a daze. Every so often she'd snap out of it and find herself at the table, drinking coffee and smoking a cigarette, with no memory of the past hour.

Even in her fog, she understood what was happening. She'd reached her limit. Her brain was shutting down. Calling it quits. Taking a break from reality. She'd hit rock bottom and wasn't ready to start climbing back up.

"Monday, nine a.m. at the federal court house across the river in White Plains. But don't get too excited yet. Have you seen the latest?"

"No. Now what?" Even to her ears, her voice sounded flat. She was resigned to the fact that until they got Roger off the road and into a hospital—or he died—each day would be more of the same. Roger on the news, in yet another town. The only that changed anymore was the background as the cameras showed him shambling past buildings and street signs.

She'd checked her phone an hour ago, there'd been nothing new. Roger and company's trek had been detoured two days earlier when storms caused damage on the Great Egg Harbor Bridge, sending the Walkers east to Ocean City, where they took Bay

Avenue South to Roosevelt Boulevard going west, which eventually brought them back to Route 9, which seemed to be their preferred route to wherever the hell it was they were headed. The same heavy wind and rain had also severely slowed their pace.

"They're in Cape May and they've left Route 9. I think you better turn on the TV."

Marcie did, switching right away to the local all news channel.

Only to discover she hadn't reached her lowest point yet after all.

But she was about to.

"What the fuck are we supposed to do?"

Alphonse Yates, who'd been elected mayor of Cape May less than a year ago, paced the short length of the meeting room. At the table sat Assistant Mayor Josephine Carlo and the three city council members, all of whom were watching the news unfold on the TV screen mounted to one wall.

"It doesn't matter," Josephine said. "We're screwed. This is about to turn into a PR nightmare."

"Tell me something I don't know," Yates muttered under his breath. The bad news was piling up and he could already imagine Carlo focusing more of her attention on how to distance herself politically from this shit pile than on how to fix it.

He couldn't blame her, either. He'd be doing the same thing in her position.

Except he wasn't in her position. Everything was landing on his shoulders.

Christ, what a monumental mess.

Those damn Walkers. Everyone had expected them to stay on Route 9 when it turned northwest. That was the road to the Cape May Ferry. What they'd do when they reached the docks was anyone's guess. Stop. Turn around. Buy two thousand goddamn tickets. He didn't care what, as long as they took their dying, controversial asses out of his town.

Instead, they'd continued south, gone over the canal bridge, and kept going right down goddamn Broadway. A parade of creepy-as-fuck pseudo-zombies, their bodies rotting and stinking to high hell with every step.

And that weird chanting. Toneless. Repeating over and over. *Walking. Walking. Walking.* God, it had been haunting his dreams since the first time he heard it.

Walking. Walking. Walking.

Yeah, they'd kept walking alright. And now they were less than three miles from the western end of Cape May Beach. After that it was five miles across the bay to Delaware.

And from the looks of things, the Walkers intended to walk their sorry asses right into the water.

Which is when the shit storm would officially turn into a hurricane.

He and the council had gone over all their options multiple times, with input from the town's attorneys. And from what Yates could see, they were truly in a damned if you do, damned if you don't situation.

If we try to stop them from entering the water, the civil rights groups will slap a lawsuit on us. There was already talk in the news of making the whole procession protected, like they were some damn religious pilgrimage. And the New York courts had, for the moment, indicated the Walkers were of sound mind and couldn't be involuntarily committed.

If we let them walk into the water and die, we're basically accomplices to murder. Had an entire town ever been accused of that? It was part of the council's—and by extension, the police's—job to keep people safe. Letting a few thousand nutjobs commit suicide was definitely going to leave a huge black stain on the town's reputation. Not to mention the whole council's political aspirations.

Aspirations? I'd be lucky to stay out of prison. And if I did, what kind of job could I find? People wouldn't trust me to walk their dogs, let alone govern their town.

What did that leave?

As far as he could see, nothing. And the rest of the council hadn't been much help, tossing around ideas that were growing increasingly preposterous. *Herd them into a holding area.* And then what? It would look like a concentration camp on the news. *Arrest them all for being public nuisances.* And where, exactly, would they put them? *Blast them with ultrasonic waves. It will disrupt their brain patterns and maybe they'll reset back to normal.* That one had come from Councilman Jane Pendergast, who'd obviously been watching too many science fiction movies. *Yeah, let me pull my sonic blaster out of my back pocket, you moron.*

Jesus, we are well and truly fucked.

Well, in that case, might as well go out in a blaze of glory.

"Okay." Yates stopped pacing and faced the council. "We can't win, so the best we can hope for is to look like we tried to do something. And in this instance, that means covering our political asses and walking the middle line."

"What the hell are you talking about, Alphonse?" Josephine asked.

"We attempt to stop them. Set up road blocks and force them north and west, into the bird sanctuary. We erect temporary fences there and say we're detaining them in the interest of their own safety. We can get our useless governor to call in the National Guard to take care of it. Then we drop the whole shit bucket in the feds' lap. We publicly demand that the governor and the president do something about this. Say it's beyond the capabilities of any town to handle, that it's gotten too far out of control and they should never have let it reach this point."

There was a moment of silence while everyone in the room considered his plan. Then Josephine shrugged.

"Fuck it. What have we got to lose?"

"Alright," Yates said. "Let's get our asses in gear. We've got a lot of calls to make and only about two hours to get this done."

As he pulled up the governor's number on his phone, Yates gave a sigh.

Goodbye, political career. It's been nice knowing you.

Marcie, along with millions of other people around the world, watched her husband die on live television.

There'd been no chance of getting from Rocky Point to Cape May before Roger and his troupe of insane believers entered the water. It was a three-hour drive with no traffic, and the news had already been saying the Walkers were less than two hours away from the shoreline and the roads were backed up or closed for miles around the whole town.

Instead, she'd sat in front of the TV, Ben and Patty with her, and followed the story as it unfolded in all its surreal glory. There was no way to avoid it even if she wanted to. Every channel had interrupted their regular broadcast to cover it. Every internet news site was showing live footage. Even radio stations were giving periodic updates in between songs.

As Roger and the others drew closer, the entire area turned into a scene of barely controlled chaos. Religious groups came out in droves, some saying it was the beginning of the apocalypse, others claiming the Walkers were the next disciples of Jesus and the waters would part before them. The Scientologists and other cults proclaimed it was the coming of this or that alien race, who would either destroy the world or save it, depending on which fake prophet you listened to.

The police barricades and National Guard troops turned out to be useless. The Walkers simply climbed over the cement barriers or squeezed between them. When they reached the soldiers, most of whom looked nervous as hell to be there, they simply kept walking until they bumped into the armed men. Without permission to use physical force, the Guardsmen were forced to step aside and let them through.

All of it accompanied by the non-stop, disturbing audio of the Walkers.

"Walking. Walking. Walking."

Thousands of bystanders flocked to the area as well, pushing and shoving to get a good look at the largest mass suicide in history.

The cameras showed Roger several times. Patty cried out and hid her face on the first occasion, and Marcie's stomach churned at the sight of his decomposing visage. Had the text under the picture not given his name, she wouldn't have even recognized him.

Nearly all of his hair had fallen out, except for a few thin strands. Patches of black marred his bone-white flesh. A bluish-gray film covered his eyes. Most of his teeth were missing. His fingernails had turned black. And still he walked on, his skeletal feet moving him steadily forward.

Many of the followers were in a similar condition. According to the reporters, those were the ones who'd joined Roger early on. The new ones showed fewer signs of trauma.

After that first time, Marcie found herself rapidly growing numb to Roger's condition. Even to the whole situation. It was like she was two separate people. One who was watching a bizarre news story unfold with an almost clinical detachment, the way you would follow any tragedy involving strangers. The other, who was becoming more distant with each moment, felt only sadness and a vague sense of loss. As if she'd lost an uncle or old college friend rather than a husband.

What husband? her mind asked. *Roger left you. Started a cult, a suicide cult like Jim Jones. He lost his mind, became a fanatic. And now he's gone. He's been gone for days.*

Her phone beeped with an incoming text. Alan Koy.

ARE YOU SEEING THIS?

She was about to text back 'what' when she noticed it.

Mixed in with the Walkers were splashes of green and brown, blue and gray. She leaned forward.

Soldiers and police officers were joining the Walkers.

A few at first. Then she counted a dozen, and then more.

And people, too. Civilians. Dressed in work clothes, bathing suits, suits and ties. One man carried a camera. On the side of it was the logo for a news outlet.

All of them walking. Their mouths moving in sync with the others.

"Walking. Walking."

The situation didn't go unnoticed, as reporters and anchors started commenting on how more and more people were joining the ranks of the Walkers.

"It's like a disease infecting anyone nearby!"

"Hundreds of people are merging into the procession."

"A woman right in front of me just dropped her purse and got in line with the Walkers. Her face, I saw it go blank."

"Connie, this is terrifying. Who will be next? Who—?"

"Frank! Get out of there! Frank!"

The shouts from the gathered throng quickly drowned out the murmuring of the Walkers. People crying out for their loved ones, their friends, their co-workers to come back. Men and women ran forward, trying to pull others from the marching cavalcade of the dead and dying. None succeeded; more than a few suddenly lost their animated expressions and began walking alongside their targets.

A gunshot went off, and then another. The shouts turned to screams and people scattered in all directions. Many fell and were trampled. Later in the day the news would report more than twenty bystanders killed and twice that many injured in the melee.

With the scene clearing, the remaining cameras had no trouble focusing on the shooters. A group of six soldiers with their rifles aimed at the Walkers. The guns went off.

Several of the Walkers stumbled or jerked to the side.

None fell.

The soldiers fired again. Somewhere off-camera a voice shouted "Cease fire!"

The soldiers ignored it. Another round went off.

A beer-bellied man in a t-shirt that said "I'm On Vacation" kept walking even as half his face exploded in a splash of red. Behind him, a teenage girl in shorts and a bikini top fell to her knees, a fist-sized hole in her belly. After a moment, she stood up and continued her trek toward the sea.

Then the gunfire stopped as more soldiers tackled their companions.

The cameras switched back to Roger. Marcie felt nothing as she watched him stride down the beach. His skeleton feet entered the water, gentle waves lapping at his ankles.

Then he was up to his knees. His waist. By then, dozens of others had waded in behind him. More and more followed.

Deeper.

His shoulders.

His chest.

His chin.

Roger's empty eye sockets, staring forward.

Hundreds in the water now.

Deeper.

Off-camera, a woman spoke in a soft, tear-choked voice.

"Dear god, this is one of the most terrible days in human history. We are witnessing something the likes of which no one has ever seen, and I pray we never see again. May god be with their souls."

The top of his skull.

Gone.

Patty and Ben leaped up from the couch and ran to their rooms.

Marcie watched for the next hour as more than five thousand people walked to their deaths.

Then she stood up, turned the TV off, and went into the kitchen, where she poured the first of many glasses of wine.

Lifting it in the air, she whispered one sentence.

"Fuck you, Roger. I hope you rot in hell."

"With us today is Doctor Ivan Khouzami." Abigail

DeClary, co-host of CNN's *Good Night to You*, gave the camera her best smile. Inside, she was seething. Out of all the people the producers could've booked, they'd found a nutcase. Bad enough she was stuck doing a midnight news program—like anyone up that late was watching the news—now she had to interview someone who had a ridiculous theory about the mass suicide in New Jersey.

I should've stayed in Buffalo doing weekend evening news. At least it had viewers.

Adding insult to injury, her co-anchor, Brett Hartley, had called in sick. Coincidentally right after the email with their guest went out.

Don't think I'll forget that, Brett. I'll find a way to get you back. I swear.

The teleprompter under the camera across the room scrolled new lines and she read them automatically.

"Doctor Khouzami is specialist in population economics, a former professor from Rutgers University, and the host of his own podcast, *The New Dawn*. Doctor Khouzami, welcome to the show."

"Thank you, Abigail." Khouzami was tall and stoop-shouldered, with an unkempt beard and equally tousled dark hair, both speckled with gray. A pair of glasses hung from his neck by a black cord. His plaid shirt and khaki pants looked like he'd slept in them. Abigail couldn't see his feet, but she felt sure he was wearing sandals with black sox. He just seemed the type.

"Doctor, you're here tonight because you have an interesting theory about the Walker phenomenon, or, as some are now calling them, the Lemmings. Please, tell us about it."

"Well, Abigail, it has to do with the ideas the Reverend Thomas Malthus, an eighteenth-century English economist who worked extensively in the field of political economy."

"Eighteenth century? Wow!" Abigail gave an exaggerated wiggle of her eyebrows as she looked at the camera, something she wished her guest would do instead of staring at her. Hadn't the backstage assistants coached him at all? "That's a long time ago. And it has bearing on what's happening today?"

"Of course. The past always infuses the future," Khouzami said, his voice dripping with condescension. Before she could interrupt him again, he continued his lecture.

"Malthus had a theory, a quite famous one, that in every society population growth eventually outpaces agricultural production, resulting in catastrophes such as war, poverty, and famine. These things force a correction in the population growth curve, essentially acting to slow growth and trigger a corresponding population decline, which will stay in effect until the population reaches a sustainable number again."

"Okay, but what does that have to do with the

Lemmings, or Walkers, whichever you prefer."

"It's quite simple when you look at the data. Like many civilizations before ours—the Romans, the Greeks, even the Mayans—our population is growing too fast. But thanks to modern technology, agricultural production is no longer the primary factor triggering a Malthusian correction. Instead, it is our own bodies and brains that are rebelling."

"What do you mean?" Abigail was surprised to find herself actually interested in the man's answer.

Khouzami placed his hands together as if praying. "Numerous studies have shown that if you put too many mice or rats in a cage, they will become super aggressive and fight to the death, even cannibalize each other, until their numbers are reduced to a sustainable level. Humans are no different. When we have small, scattered populations, we live in peace and harmony. But as those populations grow, we become more and more aggressive. We start wars over natural resources, territory, religion, anything."

He pulled a phone from his pocket and placed it on the low table between them.

"And now we have social media and the internet, perfect outlets for aggression. You see it every day. Anger, frustration, bullying. Phones and computers have become weapons instead of tools. War is no longer enough. Everything's been leading up to a major correction, something massive."

"Let me guess. The Lemming phenomenon?"

He nodded. "Exactly. Mark my words. I believe we'll see this happen again. Maybe not here. Maybe in another country. But overpopulation, altered brain functions, too many chemicals in our food… it's triggering a change in the world. The Earth isn't just a ball of rock that we inhabit. It lives, breathes, evolves. And sometimes it says enough is enough. There have been mass extinctions before. This may or may not be another, but we are certainly going to experience a transformation of some kind. A Malthusian correction, if you will."

Khouzami leaned back in his chair. Abigail did the same, a chill running down her back that she could barely hide from the camera. The man's words sounded crazy, yet…

A yellow light flashed under one of the cameras, warning her it was time for a segment break.

"Well, that was certainly fascinating, Doctor Khouzami. Thank you so much for stopping by. When we come back from our commercial break, we'll recap today's headlines. I'm Abigail DeClary, and this is *Good Night to You.*"

The camera light turned red, indicating they were off the air. She turned back to Khouzami, hoping to ask him if he would stick around so they could talk after the show.

His chair was empty.

Damn. She made a note to get his contact information from the producers.

She had more questions, and an idea that he

might make a great subject for an online interview.

Especially if his warning about more Walkers came true.

Marcie woke up the next morning with a hangover and yet with her heart surprisingly at ease. Roger's descent into the ocean had lifted an invisible but enormous weight from her, removed the yolks of guilt, fear, and sorrow from her shoulders.

With him gone, she was now free to move on with her life, begin building a new path. It would be hard, yes, but she'd escaped from the quicksand of the whole goddamn Walker disaster. Now she could focus on putting her life—and her children's—back together.

You're certainly full of metaphors this morning, aren't you?

Even the headlines in morning papers couldn't dampen her sense of relief.

HUMAN LEMMINGS COMMIT MASS
SUICIDE IN CAPE MAY!

Walkers. Lemmings. It no longer mattered to her what they were called. They were gone.

Not a single tear fell as she thought it.

By the time she fed the kids breakfast and the tutors she'd hired had arrived, two cups of coffee and some toast had chased her headache away. She showered, left a message for Alan Koy about what the next steps were for getting Roger's affairs straightened out, and then started a list of things she'd need to do. Arrange a memorial service for the family and close friends. Obtain a death certificate so she could change over the house and bank accounts into her name.

Find a job.

Part of her understood she was in a state of shock. At some point, the enormity of everything would hit her and the flood gates would open. Tears, maybe some screaming. Mourning. Grieving. All the things that came with losing a spouse.

For now, though, it was enough to be calm.

A bit of her stress returned when Alan Koy called to say that having Roger declared dead wouldn't be a problem, but they probably had a big fight ahead with the insurance company.

"They'll most likely label it as a suicide, since that's how the news keeps referring to it. That would nullify not only his life insurance, but also any death benefits from work."

"Nullify? But I was counting on those policies to hold us over until I can find work. We're talking a lot of goddamn money!"

"I know, but that's standard for all life insurance policies. I'll argue that it wasn't suicide, it was untreated mental illness. Which is a disease. We did try to have him committed. But I'm also going to file lawsuits against Rockland County for allowing him to remain free and against the town of Cape May and the states of New York and New Jersey for not only not protecting him, but preventing us from doing so. Hopefully they'll settle without a long court battle, and that will make up for the insurance money you lose. But it won't be easy or fast."

Or cheap, Marcie thought. Still, what choice did she have? She thanked Koy and hung up.

Still only one o'clock, she mused. There was a lot more to do, but exhaustion was already creeping in, a kind of mental fog more than a physical state. What she needed was a good nap.

She poured a glass of wine, went into the bedroom, and plopped onto the bed. Some mindless TV plus the alcohol would send her off nicely into dreamland. When the TV came on, it was the local news channel, which was showing an afternoon talk show.

"Welcome back to Good Afternoon Hudson Valley. Our next guest is Dr. Warren Stred, professor of animal science at the State University of New York's Rockland campus. Dr. Stred, thanks for joining us."

The perky anchor, a slim ginger with glasses Marcie felt sure were just to make her look more serious, stood and shook hands with a distinguished, slightly stooped man with snow-white hair that stood out sharply from his dark skin. Stred walked with a cane, his movements deliberate but stable. When he took the anchor's hand in his, his arm never trembled.

"Thank you, Janet," he said, taking a seat next to her. "Technically, it's Professor Emeritus. I no longer teach, but I am still head of the Animal Sciences department at the university."

"Professor Emeritus. That has a real ring to it," Janet replied, the ever-so-slight tightening of her practiced smile the only hint of her annoyance at being corrected. Then she faced the camera. "Dr. Stred is here today to talk about the Walkers. Or should we say the Lemmings, since that's what everyone's calling them now?"

Marcie laughed as the old man shook his head.

"The Lemmings. That does sound like the name of an old British band, doesn't it? The Beatles. Herman's Hermits. The Lemmings."

The host gave a weak smile that was lost as the camera switched back to Stred, who continued speaking.

"Actually, while I understand the reason for the nickname, it's not accurate at all."

"Really? Why is that?"

"Despite all the tales of lemmings killing themselves in huge numbers, they don't actually commit mass suicide. That idea got started from a Disney movie where they faked a scene of lemmings jumping off a cliff. The reality is very different."

"How so?" Janet asked, her fading interest obvious in both voice and expression. Marcie wondered if she was silently counting the minutes until she could cut to commercial. Or maybe thinking about how many people were changing channels already.

Sensationalism delivers ratings better than scientific facts.

"Lemmings will migrate when their population numbers get too large. They also happen to be good swimmers. But occasionally they'll get swept away by the current while crossing a stream or river and they drown."

"Do you think that happened with the Lemmings, er, Walkers? They thought they could cross the water but it was deeper than they realized?"

Excellent save attempt, Janet! Marcie lifted her glass in a toast.

"That's a good question. We still don't understand how the Walkers thought. They were able to answer questions when forced to. But most of the time they seemed like mindless automatons, operating on pure instinct. Like a homing pigeon returning to its nest, or geese migrating south for the winter. I have a theory, which I can't prove now since they're gone, that those people were possibly infected by some kind of fungus that affected their brains. There is an example in nature, *Ophiocordyceps unilateralis*, which is commonly known as the zombie-ant fungus. It gets into the ant's nervous system and changes the insect's behavior pattern, causing it to crawl up a plant or tree and attach itself to a twig with its mandibles. The ant remains there until the fungus blooms and bursts right out of the body. The spores are released to infect more ants. With the Walkers—"

"Thank you, Dr. Stred. That's fascinating." Janet's eyes said it was anything but. "We need to take a quick commercial break. When we come back, horror authors Jonathan Maberry and Brian Keene will help us answer the question burning in everyone's minds: were the Lemmings actual zombies?"

Oh, Christ. Now people will be calling them zombies. That's just what—

She stopped as a thought came to her. If Roger and the others were infected by a fungus, then his death couldn't be called a suicide.

Nap forgotten, she grabbed her phone to call Koy's office.

"And on the third day, he rose again!"

"Amen!"

A small crowd was gathered at Savanah Beach, Delaware, where the very reverend Nicholas Saint Paul was on his second straight day of a holy filibuster. Similar groups, some as large as forty or fifty people, others only a handful, had staked their places up and down the beaches and seaside parks along Delaware's side of the Delaware Bay. Priests, rabbis, imams, and reverends competed with men and women proclaiming to be religious leaders but who'd actually just gotten their credentials through the mail. Some didn't even have those.

Despite their differences, they were all there for the same reason: a belief that the Walkers/Lemmings would rise again from the waters, like aquatic versions of Jesus, Lazarus, the Reptilian king, or the phoenix, depending on who you listened to.

It had been three days since Roger Brenner and the others entered the bay, and there'd been no sign of them. The local police, along with the mayors of several neighboring towns, had mutually agreed to let the zealots alone and avoid any PR nightmares. Instead, officers had been placed strategically along the walkways bordering the beaches to monitor the gatherings for any signs of trouble.

"It might take three days for them to leave, or it might take seven," a police PR rep had told reporters. "It all depends on the particular ideas those nut… believers have. But when no one comes out of the water, they'll all go home. Just like those people who thought Y2K would be the end of the world."

"He shall rise and lead the righteous forward," Saint Paul shouted to his group of twelve. Half a mile down the beach, a woman in a pink muumuu was bellowing similar biblical proclamations, a cross in one hand and a donut in the other.

A handful of news vans were parked in the public lot across the street. Reporters and camera operators strolled up and down the beach, filming filler content for the nightly news and trying to get entertaining soundbites from the faithful.

"Let's call it a day." Bridget Hannah turned off her earpiece and made the traditional throat-cut motion to her camera man, Kevin Davola.

"Behold! The Chosen return!" Saint Paul's hoarse cry carried across the beach, startling several seagulls that had been foraging nearby.

Bridget sighed. The self-proclaimed reverend of the apocalypse had been shouting similar alerts throughout the morning. Each time, the crowds had stopped and turned excitedly toward the water, only to see the gray shapes of dolphins breaking the surface and disappearing again.

"Well, I'll be damned."

The normally phlegmatic Kevin's statement caught her attention more than a thousand stronger expletives. Turning, she saw nothing but sun sparkling off gentle waves.

Then she spotted it.

Or, rather, them.

Three rounded shapes emerging from the brownish-green water, a few yards out from where the waves crested in the shallows.

Another two seconds and they were identifiable as human heads. Shoulders came next, draped in seaweed. More figures appeared behind them.

The lead corpse—for there was no other way to describe it—waded forward, water spilling from what remained of its lips. Only a few patches of skin and strands of hair adorned its skull. Empty eye sockets stared straight ahead. It moved with steady intent, unfazed by the waves now lapping at its thighs. The figures behind it were in similar condition, what little flesh remaining on their bones gray with decomposition.

Bridget was about to tell Devin to turn the camera back on when she saw something that stole her ability to speak.

The lead figure wore a tattered, water-soaked zip-up hooded sweatshirt with a New York Giants emblem over the heart.

Roger Brenner. Holy fuck, he really did emerge three days later!

"Bridget. Bridget!" Someone shook her arm. Devin. He had the camera on and was pointing at her earpiece.

We're live, he mouthed.

Habit kicked in. She triggered the earpiece and stepped in front of the camera, automatically positioning herself so Devin could fit her and the emerging walkers in the frame.

"This is Bridget Hannah reporting from Savanah Beach, Delaware. And what you are witnessing can only be described as a miracle of biblical proportions. Behind me, Roger Brenner and the rest of the Walkers—we can't call them Lemmings now! —are emerging from Delaware Bay, on the third day after they entered the water in New Jersey."

"Behold the Chosen!" cried Saint Paul. "They

have arisen! The new age dawns and all sinners shall tremble!"

Devin aimed the camera at the reverend. Dozens of people were running toward him; others were swarming the beach, heading for the Walkers, who continued their emergence. Brenner and the first returnees were already trodding the sands, heading for the parking lot.

"This is surely a turning point in human history," Bridget said, as much to herself as to the camera. "I… I don't know how much of this will make the air, but we will continue to film until they are all out of the water. It is the most disturbing event I have ever seen. The Walkers stink of rot and decay. There is very little left to them. Their mouths are moving. I can hear them, it should be impossible for them to speak, but Jesus, I can hear them! Their voices, all as one, soft as the tide… they're saying, walking. Walking. And…oh, no. No, it can't be. I'm sorry, we can't stay. We have to go. Now!"

Forgetting the camera, Bridget sprinted for their van as best she could in the soft sand, Devin right behind her. On televisions across the nation, the feed showed shaking, erratic scenes that alternated between feet, sand, and parked cars. Bridget's voice could be heard shouting as they ran.

"Get out of here! Don't go near them, oh, God, don't go near them!"

Some of the bystanders heeded her advice. Others kept walking. She didn't stop. She'd seen what was happening.

Reverend Saint Paul and his followers getting in line with the Walkers. Their eyes blank, their expressions slack.

And more were joining them from up and down the beach. All of them speaking in unison.

"Walking. Walking."

"The Walkers are still heading south on Route 9."

Governor Lou Wasserman shook his head as his Chief of Staff, Shareef Rahim, moved the cursor over the map displayed on the war room wall screen.

"How many now?" he asked, wishing the damned corpses had come ashore anywhere else. Not that they could've, he reminded himself. *Lucky me, Delaware is the only state across from Jersey. Why couldn't the sharks eat them?*

"The current estimate is close to four thousand. Ever since they emerged, people have been arriving from all over the world. They're getting as close to the column of Walkers as they can, in the hopes of joining them."

"Hopes? You mean, people actually want to turn into fucking zombies?"

Joan Sabino, the Communications Director, cleared her throat. When Wasserman looked at her, she spoke.

"It's religious fervor, sir. Some of them believe

the Walkers are the chosen people, like in the Bible, and that they'll all be transported to heaven. Others think it's a sign of the apocalypse and that only the Walkers will survive it, that they'll be reborn somehow after it's over to rebuild a new society on Earth."

"Don't forget the space people," muttered Sinclair Tooms, the Lieutenant Governor.

"Right. There's a whole group that believe when the Walkers finally get to wherever they're going, space ships will land and take them away."

"Jesus Christ. The whole world is going crazy." Wasserman ran his hand through his luxuriously thick silver hair. That mane had helped him get elected over his bald, stout opponent. Survey after survey had indicated it gave him a distinguished look that made people want to trust him. Now it was disheveled and greasy from a long, frustrating day.

The Walker situation was now officially a state emergency. Route 9 was impassible for cars; the damn corpses were taking up the lanes in both directions. Troopers, local police, and the National Guard had all been called upon to route traffic along multiple detours, many of which were now clogging up as more and more nutcases—along with eager media and science teams from around the globe—arrived.

In short, it had turned into a complete cluster fuck with no end in sight until—

"Wait." Wasserman turned toward the screen.

"They're sticking to Route 9, right?" He didn't wait for confirmation. "That only goes so far before it joins with Route 13, which is the one road they can take if they want to keep moving south. We're talking about what, thirty, thirty-five miles from Lewes to where they'd cross over into Maryland at Delmar?"

"Thirty-seven," Sabino said, checking her phone.

Wasserman nodded, a plan unfolding as he spoke. "Thirty-seven. And the Walkers are averaging two miles an hour. And they've already been walking for six hours. That means less than a day before they reach the Maryland border, and maybe another hour or two for the whole mess of them to cross over it. And after that, guess what? It's no longer our goddamn problem. So here's what we do. We've already enacted a state of emergency, which means we can pretty much do whatever the fuck we want. And what I want is to shut the whole damn state down."

"What?" The Lieutenant Governor shot up from his chair. "You can't do that!"

"The hell I can't. We did it during COVID. The precedent is already there. Shelter in place. It's just one day. That's all. Every non-essential person stays home for one day. Then tomorrow morning it's business as usual and we can let Jack McCarthy in Maryland deal about it."

"No, it won't work." Tooms stood up, his eyes wide. "The people—"

"Actually, it might work." Joan Sabino raised her voice enough to interrupt Tooms, who glared at her but sat down. "Like the Governor said, we have precedent. And we can say it's for two reasons: public safety and public health. We don't know what kind of diseases those corpses carry. I'll get the state Surgeon General's office to back us up."

"Perfect!" Wasserman slapped his hand on the table. "Get to work. By this time tomorrow, our problems will be over."

For Marcie, the Walkers' submersion and ensuing emergence produced a series of unexpected consequences. On the negative side, her life was thrown into the spotlight again as Roger once more became the number one news story in the world. It was impossible to watch TV or go on social media without seeing his rotting corpse and the growing legion of dead following him south. The media had again taken to camping out on her street, forcing her and the kids to lock themselves inside with the curtains drawn. Both Ben and Patty spent nearly all their time in their rooms. On the rare occasions they emerged, they were sullen and non-communicative. She feared the family was nearing their breaking point.

On the positive side, Alan Koy had managed to get all charges against her dropped except for disorderly conduct, which only carried a fine. Even better, two days after the so-called "Return" Benjamin Thoma called her with the best news she'd had since the day Roger took off.

"I hope you're sitting down, Marcie," he said, "because I just heard from the insurance company. They're going to pay on Roger's policies."

"What? Are you serious? Why? How much?" The questions tumbled out as her mind whirled. Money! Finally there would be some money coming in. Her job search had been fruitless thanks to the dreadful publicity surrounding her name, and their bank account was nearing depletion.

"All of it. Every last dime. You should have the checks in a week. Same for his death benefits from work."

Marcie dropped onto the sofa, her entire body going weak. Both policies! Roger had insisted that they each carry two, one to take care of the house and bills, one to pay for the kids' college tuitions and set up the survivor for early retirement. The total value of his policies was…

Almost two million dollars.

The number kept repeating in her head. She was vaguely aware of Thoma explaining what had happened. The fungal infection theory hadn't panned out; a sample taken by a CDC team had been unable to culture anything unusual, or even harmful. However, they had publicly hypothesized that a virus could be the culprit, based on the rapid change that happened to so many of the people who came in contact with the Walkers. One of the scientists even referred to Roger as 'patient zero.'

"That, combined with the fact that Roger is still walking and sort of talking forced the insurance company's hand," Thoma said. "Turns out to be a real catch twenty-two for them. Roger obviously isn't alive, but they can't say he committed suicide if he's still walking around. This will put a lot of insurance companies out of business before it's over. We're lucky to be cashing in before the crash."

Then he delivered even bigger news.

He wouldn't be charging her for the work he'd done.

As it turned out, several other Walkers' families had hired him to represent them in their insurance cases, so he was writing off Marcie's bill as a thank you.

Two million dollars. After she hung up the phone, she sat with her eyes closed, just basking in the sense of liberation those three words delivered.

Two million dollars.

What would she do?

Her lips slowly curled up in a smile as another thought appeared on the heels of the last one.

Anything I goddamn want.

Her smile turned into laughter as she realized that for the first time since Roger walked out the door, she was truly free.

Roger had ruined the life she had built with him, run her right off the road they'd planned on following right into retirement.

But now that same detour had put her on a new road, one with endless possibilities.

And she intended to take it.

From Maryland to Virginia, the Walkers remained on Route 13, picking up more followers with each mile. By the time they crossed the Chesapeake Bay Bridge and reached Norfolk, their numbers had swelled to almost nine thousand. When they reached the border of North Carolina a day later, the Walkers were well over twenty thousand strong and their shambling parade was nearly nine miles long.

North Carolina's governor, Norbert Sullivan, had the National Guard waiting for them with orders to shoot for the head the moment they crossed the state line.

Ten minutes before Roger Brenner walked past a sign that read Welcome to North Carolina, the President of the United States called him personally to order the troops to stand down. He was declaring the Walkers protected, and no violence against them would be allowed.

"Close the roads, put up barriers, do whatever you have to in order to protect your citizens from getting too close. But I want to make sure this is perfectly clear. You *will* let them pass through your state unharmed."

For a good thirty seconds, Sullivan, who'd campaigned aggressively against the POTUS in the last election, considered ignoring the order and blasting the Walkers into oblivion, presidential decrees and religious beliefs be damned.

Then he remembered his own voting base, many of whom were loudly proclaiming this the greatest miracle since the coming of Christ.

"Yes, sir," he said into the phone. He made sure to close the connection before turning to Major Poncrieff of the North Carolina National Guard, who stood next to him in the temporary war room of the state capitol building and had heard the whole conversation. They shared an eye-roll before Sullivan grudgingly gave the order to stand down.

When the crowds gathered at the border began to cheer as the Walkers crossed over, Sullivan couldn't take it anymore and turned off the TV.

Such was his shame that later that evening he used one of the back exits so he wouldn't have to walk past the statues of Polk, Jackson, and Johnson, the three great presidents who'd come from North Carolina. Men who'd never allow an army of the dead to sully their great state.

By the time the Walkers reached South Carolina five days later, they were three quarters of a million strong and still growing. They left in their wake a disaster worse than any hurricane to ever hit North

Carolina, one that forced Governor Sullivan to visit the White House hat in hands and beg for federal aid. The massive shutdowns of roads and businesses took an enormous toll on the economy.

In South Carolina, preparations were hastily made. Emergency plans based on those used during the pandemic were instituted, including shelter in place orders for the entire Interstate 95 corridor, which had become the Walkers' road of choice after Route 13 turned west back in Goldsboro.

Having a fifteen-mile-long army of the walking dead occupy the main travel route through the Carolinas not only disrupted the commerce of both states, but also the eastern seaboard, as it caused massive delays in shipments moving in both directions.

This, in turn, forced the President to declare a national state of emergency, something his opponents said he should've done back when the Walkers were in Virginia.

Much like the governors of New Jersey, North Carolina, and South Carolina, President Carson Wallace watched the dead march across his country and take all hopes of re-election with them.

Roger Brenner existed, although not in a way comprehensible to living humans.

Aware, yet not. Thinking, yet not.

The remnants of brain matter still enduring

inside his skull were nothing but a soupy mixture of dead cells. The only flesh remaining on his body were the tendons and ligaments holding his bones together.

Yet somehow he walked. He retained his balance, moved his limbs. Understood, at a very basic level, where he was in relation to his surroundings. Maintained an awareness of all the other Walkers following him, and the ones who were yet to arrive. Knew when to turn, when to continue straight, how to continue orienting himself south. The destination he'd spoken of but never named, back when he had the power of speech, shined like a beacon in what passed for a kind of antediluvian consciousness. His jaw moved up and down, and if someone were close enough, they would hear a whispering of air moving through the spaces between the bones.

Whoossshhhh-shsssh. Whoossshhhh-shsssh.

Walking. Walking.

The Walkers hit the million person milestone just west of Charleston, South Carolina. Several media outlets declared them a diaspora, causing an outcry from numerous countries stating the dead were not a race or culture. A self-proclaimed political group, the People for a New State, set up protests along I95, demanding the undead had rights and the Walkers should be granted their own independent state wherever they eventually stopped.

In Mexico, Guatemala, Cuba, and Nicaragua, government officials began planning for the possible arrival of the Walkers should they decide to cross the Gulf of Mexico or the short stretch of ocean at the tip of Florida.

Not long after the estimate of one million was announced, a woman in San Francisco got up from the lunch table at work and stated she 'had to go.' Her co-workers paid no attention until they noticed her empty desk a couple of hours later.

She was next seen walking southeast on Route 101 toward Palo Alto. By the time she reached the city limits, there were more than fifty Walkers following her.

At the same time, a group of high school seniors in Minneapolis stood up in the middle of history class, left the class without a word, exited the building, and headed south on Interstate 35. It only took an hour before other men, women, and children began to join them on their trek.

All of them were smiling and repeating the words, walking, walking.

It wasn't lost on the press or the scientists studying the phenomenon that all of the new Walkers were speaking in precise time to Roger Brenner's mouth movements.

Within hours, Walkers were reported in Bogota, London, Paris, Munich, Mexico City, Hong Kong, Taipei, Beijing, Tokyo, and Moscow.

Government heads and military leaders accused

each other of releasing an experimental bioweapon. Russia and China threatened war against the U.S., who in turn promised swift and furious retaliation. Several countries shut down their borders and called out their military, only to see huge numbers of soldiers drop their weapons, abandon their posts, and join the ranks of the Walkers.

Scientific teams in biohazard suits were sent to obtain samples, only to discover that whatever the cause of the Walker transformation was, it had nothing to do with airborne or physical transmission.

Various subject matter experts from the fields of virology and epidemiology proclaimed people should stay as far from any Walkers as possible. The United Nations and the World Health Organization called for a global quarantine, a stricter 'shelter inside' than ever before enacted.

However, when it became known that people who were dozens, even hundreds of miles from the nearest Walker group were falling victim to the phenomenon, the governments rescinded all the recommendations. With the economic disaster of the COVID-19 pandemic still fresh in their minds, presidents, dictators, kings, and queens all unanimously decided it was better to ride out wave of supernatural conscription and then carry on as best as possible in its wake.

The harsh reality was, nothing anyone did made a difference.

New outbreaks of Walkers kept popping up, usually in larger cities but also in nearby suburbs.

Trickles of Walkers emerged from these miniature hotspots to join up with the larger hordes like tributaries meeting rivers.

Three days after the events in San Francisco and Minneapolis, the number of Walkers in the U.S. totaled more than three million, and an estimated forty million had joined the ranks worldwide.

All of them making their way through populous areas and apparently heading toward large bodies of water.

"Hello, and welcome to a special edition of Good Night to You. With us tonight once again is Doctor Ivan Khouzami, our resident specialist in population economics and host of his highly popular podcast, The New Dawn. Doctor Khouzami, welcome back to our show."

Abigai DeClary made it a point to look from the camera to Khouzami and then back again. Every second of screen time counted tonight; thanks to the global Walker pandemic, Khouzami's fringe theories about Malthusian population correction and a living Earth had thrust him and his podcast into the spotlight, and that meant big ratings whenever he appeared on a program. Big enough that CNN had given her an elite time slot, seven o'clock on a Sunday night, to conduct her second interview with him. An interview he'd at first refused to do, until he was informed he had no choice. His contract for the first appearance stated quite clearly that CNN had the right to do a follow-up with him if they chose.

And goddamn it, Abigail sure as hell chose yes on that one.

This time there'd be an estimated nine million viewers watching her. Nine million! Her head spun just thinking about it. She'd donned a new blue dress, one that looked smartly professional yet showed just a hint of cleavage, gotten her hair done in a serious yet flattering style that framed her face perfectly, and spent an hour in the makeup chair to ensure she looked flawless but not plastic on camera.

This was maybe her best—and possibly last—chance to grab a prime time news anchor job, and she wasn't going to blow the audition.

"Thank you, Abigail, happy to be back." Khouzami's tone indicated he was anything but pleased to be there. The producers had literally threatened to sue him for breach of contract if he didn't appear.

Tough luck, fella. Should've read before you signed.

"Well, I think it's an understatement to say a lot has happened since the last time we spoke. Is it your opinion that the recent events have substantiated your theory about the reason for the Walker phenomenon?"

"Of course." Khouzami leaned forward, his

stooped, gangly form and oversized, curved nose giving him the appearance of a vulture perched in a tree. His graying beard and hair appeared even more unkempt than before, and she was positive he still wore the same rumpled plaid shirt and khakis as his last visit.

"As I've stated all along, the Earth has undergone population corrections on multiple occasions, going all the way back to before the time of the dinosaurs. This is simply another example of the Malthusian effect happening on a global scale rather than in a small, localized population of animals. We've reached the tipping point and now the correction has begun in earnest."

"So it's your belief that somehow the Earth itself, a planet, is actually controlling this correction? That our world is, in a way, alive?"

"Not 'in a way.' It *is* alive, just not in the manner we are used to seeing or imagining. Life doesn't require a beating heart or breathing lungs. It doesn't need to eat or drink. Our distant ancestors had the right idea when they worshipped our planet. The Greeks called her Gaia, the Earth Goddess. There is a Hindu sect that celebrates the Ambubachi Mela, an annual fertility festival involving the Earth-Woman's menstruation cycle. The Neolithic people of Europe called her the Earth Mother, and that idea lasted for thousands of years, right down to the Celtic and Druid cultures of Ireland, Scotland, and England. A belief that the Earth is alive and we are simply part of her is neither new nor outlandish, as some continue to insist, despite the latest evidence to the contrary."

"Wow. That's quite a theory." Abigail flashed another thousand-watt smile at the camera before returning her attention to her guest, who was frowning. "Assuming you're correct, what do you think will happen next?"

A glimmer of malicious delight appeared in Khouzami's eyes, and his lips twitched up in a hint of a smile, one that gave Abigail the impression he enjoyed delivering bad news. Or at least this bad news.

"As I've said on my own podcast, there can be only one outcome. The Walkers will converge in places where they can carry out their final exit. Every exodus has a purpose and a destination. We know the purpose of the Walkers: to decrease the burden mankind places on the Earth. What we can't be sure of is their destination. However, based on the trajectories of the various groups, it is my belief that they will all end their journeys in the oceans, where they will be consumed and their molecules be recycled for the Earth to use again."

"Consumed, as in eaten? You're saying that the Walkers really are like lemmings, committing a mass suicide? That all those people who are, or were, living, breathing human beings, are just going to offer themselves up as food for this Earth Mother you believe in?"

Now Khouzami's smile went from subtle to blatant and his expression was full of malicious joy.

"That's all any of us are, Abigail. We exist only to feed Gaia. Anything else—our lives, our dreams, our thoughts and hopes—is just incidental. We are crops for her. We grow, we die, and our nutrients are returned to her to start over. But modern society has disrupted that cycle. We remove nutrients and water from her but we don't return them. Buildings of concrete and steel do not rot away like wood. Bodies filled with formaldehyde sitting in metal caskets do not decompose as they should. We rob her of what she needs, and at the same time we overgrow the land, taking more than our fair share of resources. At some point, we became weeds rather than crops. Or, to put it another way, we're like an infection of the gut, where a species of bacteria suddenly proliferates because the balance is changed, and it goes from being beneficial to virulent. And just like our bodies do, Mother Nature is expelling the cause of the illness. Those people aren't lemmings. They're bacteria, and the Earth is shitting them out."

Abigail leaned back, dimly aware of the camera's yellow light and her wide-eyed assistant producer behind it, making a throat-cutting motion at her. Screw that. This was too good to stop for some inane dog food or soap commercial. He'd just compared mankind to germs and said the Walker phenomenon was Earth experiencing a case of

Montezuma's revenge.

This could very well be Emmy material, especially if he turned out to be right.

"That is… that is very grim, Doctor Khouzami. But in your hypothesis, is that all? The Earth makes this big Mal, er, Malthuson—"

"Malthusian," he said, his brows furrowing at the mistake.

"Malthusian correction, and then everything goes back to normal?"

"Normal?" Khouzami let out a snort of laughter. "Nothing is ever going to be normal again. This is just the beginning. A few million people is nothing to Gaia. If we don't learn our lesson and change how we treat this planet, well, let's just say we should get our affairs in order. And remember the Bible."

"The Bible? What does—"

"It's all there. Genesis Six-Nine. Isaiah Twenty-Four Eighteen. Corinthians Fifteen-Fifty-Two. Peter Three-Ten. They remembered the old stories, the ones passed down from the times before recorded time. People call them fables. They don't want to believe. Their eyes are closed to the truth. But soon they will know. Soon everyone will. And by then it will be too late, there will be nothing they can do to stop what's coming."

Khouzami leaned back and crossed his arms over his chest, clearly happy to end things on a chilling note.

Abigail looked at the camera. The assistant producer's expression was frantic and he appeared ready to storm the set and force a commercial break.

"Thank you, Doctor Khouzami. That was… that was something. Let's take a break and hear from our sponsors. When we come back, we'll be speaking with Dave Simmons, host of Economy Today, about the economic fallout of the Walker crisis."

The camera light went red and Abigail let out a sigh. She was surprised to see Khouzami hadn't walked off this time. He still sat in his chair, staring at her. His eyes held a malevolent gleam that sent a shiver down her back.

"Thank you for having me on again, Ms. DeClary," he said, and then he stood up. "I do hope you'll survive the Great Correction."

"Well, so do I! Cross my fingers for good luck." She made the gesture with both hands, a habit she'd had since childhood.

He shook his head, his smile growing wider.

"Good luck? Oh, no. Just the opposite. Those who survive will definitely wish they hadn't."

Twenty-six days after departing his house in Rocky Point, Roger Brenner led more than two-and-a-half million Walkers across Cedar Key, Florida, following Florida State Road 24 to where it became D Street and continued on through town to the

Gulf of Mexico, where hundreds of news crews waited. The Walkers crossed First Street just as the first hint of the morning sun lightened the sky. The entire waterfront section of Cedar Key had been ordered to evacuate or shelter in place the previous day. Those who'd chosen to stay were able to hear the clackity-click of bones striking each other from a mile away even with the windows closed, as millions of unliving skeletons advanced down the road.

"Like if you took everyone in town and told them to strike drumsticks together," one resident described it later to a reporter.

"It was so loud, woke me from my sleep," another person said. "God help me, I've never heard anything so awful in my life. I'll have nightmares forever, that's fer sure."

"It was the eternal drumming of the dead," said an old Black woman, and it was her quote that went viral within hours.

Roger, his teeth clicking together as he wordlessly recited his mantra, stepped off the walkway and onto the sand while myriad cameras, including overhead drones, recorded the historic event. He entered the water and continued forward until he disappeared from sight. Behind him came the rest of the Walkers in their lemming-like fashion, a procession of the dead and dying that continued chanting "Walking, walking," until the last of them vanished beneath the blue-green water precisely twenty-four hours after Roger's sun-bleached bones first touched the shoreline.

For the rest of the night, field reporters, anchorpeople, and pundits vied for soundbites. In the end, it was an aging correspondent from Buffalo who delivered an Emmy-winning line when, with the rising sun a fiery red ball behind him, he closed his account with a single sentence:

"As the sun rises behind me, I can't help but wonder if this isn't just the dawn of a new day, but of a new reality for mankind."

Twenty miles out and more than three hundred feet down, Roger Brenner came to a stop as the force guiding him signaled him to stop. He'd reached his destination. His head tilted back and his empty sockets stared up at the distant surface.

A single thought came to him as his consciousness was returned to him for one final time.

Goodbye, Marcie, Patty, Ben. Be well. I love you.

The supernatural power keeping him together released its hold and his bones disarticulated, falling into a pile on the sea floor.

As each Walker reached him, the same thing happened.

By the time the last one arrived, they had formed the largest human graveyard in existence.

Until the first Chinese Walkers reached the Philippine Sea.

"The President has announced he is terminating the national state of emergency based on the absence of any further Walker clusters being reported in the United States. Elsewhere, the last of the clusters in Africa and South America have entered the Atlantic Ocean. Tonight he will deliver a special State of the Union address regarding the nation's recovery efforts in the wake of the tremendous economic toll the Walkers—"

Marcie Brenner hit the remote to change the channel. Another news story came on, showing a group of Walkers wading into the ocean at a Rio de Janeiro beach. She scrolled to the next station, was rewarded with a perky blonde showing too much cleavage smiling brightly at the camera. Behind her was a picture of a sixty-something-year-old man with an unkempt beard and hair, an oversized nose, and wrinkled clothes.

"—And in other news, Doctor Ivan Khouzami, who I interviewed twice during the height of the Walker catastrophe, has been arrested. He has been charged by the New Jersey State Attorney General's Office for making claims designed to incite public imminent lawless action. In her statement to the press, Assistant Attorney General Lewellyn White mentioned assertions Khouzami made on his podcast that the only way to save the world is to overthrow society as we know it and return to a naturalist way of life—"

"Jesus, save us from the crazies." Marcie turned off the TV and looked at the clock on the cable box. Eleven forty-five. Almost noon. Definitely not too early for a drink.

She went to the wet bar and poured a glass of Riesling. Wine in one hand and phone in the other, she headed out to the balcony, which overlooked the Pacific Ocean at Sunset Cliffs in San Diego. The two-bedroom apartment had cost her half the insurance settlement, but it was worth it. Just like the two thousand she'd spent changing their last name back to her maiden name of Waterson. Starting a new life was the best decision she'd ever made. The kids were happy and attending school again, already making new friends. She'd found herself a part-time job doing bookkeeping for a bakery. It was only three days a week, but that, plus the interest from the million still in the bank, was enough to keep them in food, clothes, and booze until she found something better. And there were the book and interview offers Alan Koy was reviewing. If they panned out, she might never have to work again.

And I have this view every day, she thought, settling herself onto one of the deck chairs. Down on the beach, the last of the morning's surfers were packing up their boards and heading for the taco or seafood stands for lunch and early happy hours.

She'd been pretty certain San Diego would be a great place to live, but she hadn't expected that she and the kids would fall madly in love with it so quickly. They'd only been there a month and it already seemed like home.

All because my husband became the leader of some supernatural mass suicide. Who'd have thought him ruining our lives would also be the best thing to ever happen to us?

"Thank you, Roger," she said, lifting her glass. "Goodbye and good riddance. Here's to a new and better life."

She toasted the air and then sipped. No more Roger. No more embarrassing Brenner name. And now no more Walkers.

"Life is good," she said, smiling as she set the glass down on the little outdoor table and picked up her phone. Time for some retail therapy. She'd seen a cute outfit on a site that—

The balcony vibrated softly under her feet and a low rumble, more felt than heard, reached her. At first she thought it might be some kind of large construction truck down on the street but it quickly grew stronger, shaking the table so badly she had to grab her wine before it toppled over. The vibration grew into a shuddering. Inside the apartment, glasses fell and shattered. Twelve stories down, car alarms shrieked in electronic terror.

The rumbling grew louder, drowning out the morning sounds.

Earthquake!

She'd known California was prone to them, but there'd never been so much as a mild tremor since they'd moved into the apartment.

She tried to remember what she was supposed to do. Get inside? Hide in the tub or under a table?

Marcie stood up, and as she did she heard screaming from the beach. Looking down, she saw the ocean receding rapidly from the shore, exposing first dozens and then hundreds of yards of wet sand, seaweed, and then a sharp drop-off into darkness. A few sailboats and jet skis were left stranded on rock-strewn sand where normally the water was well over twenty feet deep.

In the distance, a tall, white line of water rose up.

Somewhere in town, emergency sirens wailed.

Marcie turned and ran for the bathroom. Her last thought before the tsunami struck the building was not for her own safety, or even her children's.

Damn you Roger. This is all your fault.

On the other side of the country, in the interrogation room of a Princeton, New Jersey police station, Ivan Khouzami looked up at the camera, smiled, and mouthed three words.

"Mother is angry."

About the Author

JG FAHERTY is the author of 25 books, 4 collections, and more than 85 short stories. Born and raised in New York's haunted Hudson Valley and now a resident of North Carolina's equally haunted Cape Fear region, he writes adult and YA horror, science fiction, dark fantasy, and paranormal romance, and his works range from quiet, dark suspense to over-the-top comic gruesomeness. He's been a finalist for both the Bram Stoker Award (twice) and ITW Thriller Award, and is proud to be a relative of Mary Shelley. You can follow him at www.twitter.com/jgfaherty, www.facebook.com/jgfaherty, www.instagram.com/jgfaherty, and www.jgfaherty.com.

Also from JG Faherty and Lycan Valley

Available in ebook, audiobook and paperback from LycanValley.com

www.ingramcontent.com/pod-product-compliance
Lightning Source LLC
Chambersburg PA
CBHW010737100726
47899CB00009B/3093